Amish
Acres

The

Pumpkin Patch

Samantha Bayarr

Amish Acres: The Pumpkin Patch

Amish Acres: Book Three: The Pumpkin Patch

Copyright © 2018 by Samantha Bayarr

This is a work of fiction. Names, characters, places, and incidents are the product of the author's imagination. Locales and public names are sometimes used for atmospheric purposes. Any resemblance to actual people, living or dead, or any business, events, or locations is entirely coincidental, and beyond the intent of the author.

<u>GLOSSARY</u>

ach: oh

aenti: aunt

boppli: baby

brudder: brother

danki: thank you

dat: father, dad

dawdi: grandfather

dochder: daughter

dummkopf: dumb

Englisher: a person who is not Amish

Fraa: wife

Frau: married woman

Freinden: friends

Gude mariye: good morning

gut: good

haus: house

jah: yes

kaffi: coffee

kapp: prayer cap

kinner: children

kume: come

mei: my

mamm: mom, mother

narrish: crazy, foolish

naerfich: nervous

onkel: uncle

Ordnung: rules of the Amish faith

Schweschder: sister

Wilkum: welcome

A NOTE FROM THE AUTHOR

While this story is set against the real backdrop of an Amish community, the characters and the town are fictional. There is no intended resemblance between the characters and community in this story and any real members of the Amish or communities. As with any work of fiction, I've taken license in some areas of research as a means of creating the necessary circumstances for my characters and the community in which they live. My research and experience with the Amish are quite knowledgeable; however, it would be impossible to be entirely accurate in details and description since every community differs, and I have not lived near enough to an Amish community for several years to know pertinent and current details.

Therefore, any inaccuracies in the Amish lifestyle and their community portrayed in this book are due to fictional license as the author.

Dedicated to my readers

Thank you for downloading this book. My purpose is to entertain you for a little while and to help you forget the troubles of life while you lose yourself in the pages of this story.

Sit back and relax with your favorite cup of herbal tea or coffee and get lost in the pages of the fictitious world I've created just for you—the reader.

Happy Reading and have a blessed life

CHAPTER ONE

RUTHIE Yoder swung her feet over the edge of her bed, shivering in the cold room. The wood floor was so cold it made her feet ache and she wondered if there had been an early frost. While her sister, Naomi, had been busy discovering who planted the celery patch on their property, Ruthie had taken a more practical approach to her time and had planted a large pumpkin patch. Now that it was nearing the end of October, she planned to get the harvest of pumpkins into town for an end-of-season sale at Murdock's Farmer's Market in the town square. Most of the pumpkins were decorative gourds and would serve the *Englishers* well, while a third of her patch consisted of pie pumpkins. She would use those to make bread, muffins, cookies, and pies to sell at her market post. This would be her first year bringing her wares to market, and they would need the extra money over the winter months. Her cousin, Beth, had suggested she bring some of them to the autumn festival their community puts on at the end of harvest to get ready for wedding season.

With Naomi busy planning her wedding that would take place in only a few weeks, and *Dat* being as tired as he was all the time after he finished his chores, she knew she was on her own—especially since Jacob had left for his *rumspringa* as soon as he had his birthday. He'd been the one she thought she would marry, but he was eager to leave her behind when she'd declined to go with him. Since the news had quickly spread in the community of Annie's pregnancy, and there was some talk about the timing of the announcement and their wedding, Ruthie was content to stay home where she was needed. The last thing she wanted to do was to end up pregnant so young like Annie.

It was just as well; Naomi needed her here to help with her wedding, and her pumpkin patch was not going to pick itself. The timing was not right for her to go away on *rumspringa;* she wasn't sure if it ever would be. With Naomi leaving *Dat* to marry Jeremiah, she was needed at home—for the time-being.

Ruthie stretched and yawned, rising from her bed to begin her day. The sun was still low enough in the sky that a blue glow streamed in through her window, providing enough light for her to get dressed.

Maybe I can twist Beth's arm into helping me!

She pulled on a pair of warm stockings, which she was certain she would be peeling off before the day was over; this time of year it was cold at night and in the morning, but by afternoon, she'd be sweating from the heat. Donning her work apron, Ruthie went downstairs to make a pot of coffee before Naomi got up. She'd been out late with her betrothed nearly every night this week, and so the making of breakfast had fallen upon Ruthie. She would have to do it every day once Naomi was living with Jeremiah in their new house he built, so she did the chore without grumbling. At least she still had help with the evening meal and most of the chores; she was grateful for that much.

Ruthie gazed out the kitchen window as she filled the coffee pot with tap water. The barn door was open, and her father would likely be inside soon with a pail of milk. She struck a match and turned the knob to the gas stove and lit the burner. She yawned as she scooped the coffee into the percolator basket and then placed it inside the pot and replaced the lid. Her mind drifted to her pumpkin patch as she set the iron skillet on the back burner and placed strips of bacon in it. She would make scrambled eggs today because they were fastest, and it would assure she would get out of the house on time to make it downtown before the sun became too warm. The heat would make unloading her buggy almost unbearable.

Naomi came into the kitchen, her slippers shuffling across the floor. The coffee had barely begun to percolate, and she walked over to the stove and groaned.

"How much longer till it's ready?" she asked, flipping her long braid over her shoulder.

"Another late night with your beau, I see," Ruthie teased. "Do you plan to get dressed today?"

Naomi shrugged. "Not if I can help it; I had no idea planning a wedding was such hard work. We could have talked all night about the arrangements and still not come close to settling everything. We're running out of time, and we still have so much to do."

"I hope you plan on doing your chores today," Ruthie said. "I have to take my pumpkins into town to sell. All next week I have to spend every minute baking for the festival on Saturday."

Naomi sank into the nearest chair and laid her head down on the table and groaned. "I still haven't started on my dress; I was hoping to at least get the fabric cut this weekend since it's not a church weekend."

Ruthie poured Naomi a cup of coffee and set it in front of her. "Perhaps if you didn't stay out so late with Jeremiah every night, you'd get it done on time."

Naomi took a long sip of her coffee and sighed. "I'll need about four cups of this to get me going this morning," she said.

Ruthie laughed at her sister's comment and went about cracking the eggs for breakfast. "You better get dressed before *Dat* sees you," she warned.

Naomi shuffled over to the stove and topped off her coffee cup and then left the kitchen.

Scrambling the eggs with a whisk, Ruthie peered out the window at Seth, who'd just pulled into the yard driving a flatbed wagon full of hay bales for her father. Her heart quickened when a thought popped into her head. She cracked four extra eggs into the bowl knowing her father would invite him into the house to share the meal with them. Thankful she'd made an extra loaf of banana bread yesterday morning, she turned on the oven to warm it so they could have it with their breakfast. After turning the bacon, she buttered the bottom of the large skillet and lit the burner, turning the flame to medium-low so the eggs wouldn't scorch before *Dat* and Seth came in from the barn. Then she sliced the honeydew melon she'd brought up from the cellar the night before and placed it in the fridge to keep cool. Everything had to be just right for her to get Seth in just the right mood, and a full belly was the best way to make a man happy. Timing had to be just right, or Naomi would spoil it for her. She'd wait until her sister excused herself to go over to her new house to finish her curtains, and then she'd present her request to Seth.

Seth put the last bale of hay in the barn for Mr. Yoder after accepting his offer to take the evening meal with him and his daughters. He was over the misunderstanding between him and Naomi after their *almost* kiss. In the end, he realized that his cousin, Jeremiah, was the best man for her. After all, he didn't love Naomi; he'd had a crush on her since they were in school together and hadn't realized until he tried to kiss her that he'd spent a lot of years building up the crush in his mind. They were no more compatible than he would have been with Annie Lapp. His chances of finding a wife were dwindling with each wedding season that passed him by, his prospects becoming slimmer every day. He'd been in no hurry to marry until all his friends and cousins his age had suddenly decided this was the last wedding season they would see come and go without matching up with someone. After his discovery about Naomi not being the one for him, he'd put it out of his mind altogether, trusting that God would surely bring his bride to him when he was least expecting her.

Seth followed Mr. Yoder into the house, the scent of warm banana bread making his mouth water. It was his favorite, and he could eat a whole loaf slathered in butter all by himself. But then his nose detected bacon and freshly-brewed coffee, and he knew he was in for a breakfast that would leave him plenty satisfied.

He and Mr. Yoder finished washing in the mudroom sink and removed their hats, placing them on the pegs near the door. They entered the kitchen where Ruthie was busy at the stove dishing up scrambled eggs into a dish. She turned when they sat at the table and smiled at her father first and then at Seth. His heart did a funny flip behind his ribcage, and he felt his cheeks warm at her friendly gesture.

She brought the covered dish full of eggs to the table and a plate full of bacon, setting them both in the center. She busied herself pouring her father a cup of coffee and then raised her eyes casually at him.

"*Kaffi?*" she asked with another smile that made his heart thump.

He stared at her, wondering why he'd never noticed her before now.

"Seth; do you want *kaffi?*" Ruthie repeated, interrupting his reverie.

He cleared his throat, feeling his cheeks warm with embarrassment.

"*Jah,*" he answered, his throat cracking just a bit.

She smiled at him again and poured him a cup of coffee. Had she always smiled at him when conversing with him, or had this been the first time he'd really noticed her? She'd always just been Naomi's little sister—too young for him, except that she'd recently had a birthday, making her eligible for marriage. Being that he was almost four years older than she was, he felt it was scandalous that he should be sitting across from her father entertaining thoughts of marrying the young woman simply because she'd smiled at him.

What is wrong with me today?

"*Danki,*" Seth said when she'd finished pouring the coffee into his cup.

She placed the pot on a trivet on the table and then brought a loaf of banana bread and sliced melon to the table. After setting them down, she sat in the chair next to Seth, and her father reached for her hand and bowed his head to say the prayer. Ruthie reached for Seth's hand, sending shivers all the way up his arm, and he was grateful for the chance to close his eyes and bow his head for the prayer. Before Mr. Yoder began his prayer, Naomi sat on the other side of Seth, and he barely noticed when she'd pulled his other hand in hers automatically. Seth gulped, unable to ignore the heat he felt in Ruthie's touch as she clasped her fingers around his. How was he going to get through the meal sitting so close to Ruthie with the crazy thoughts rolling in his head about her?

CHAPTER TWO

RUTHIE couldn't help but sense Seth squirming next to her as her father had said the prayer; he'd been acting strange since he'd walked into the house. He'd hesitated when she'd asked him about the coffee, and he'd even had a tough time keeping up with his conversation with her father. Now that the prayer had ended, he hadn't let go of her hand underneath the table, and it tickled Ruthie just a bit to wonder if he might just be fond of her. Surely, he'd heard that she'd had a birthday. She knew he was older than she was by a few years, but that didn't bother her; Seth was handsome and a hard worker.

She held out her plate with her left hand to her father as he dished the eggs; though she and Naomi made the meals, he'd always served them at the table before filling his own plate. It wasn't the way most families in the community did things; normally, the women did all the serving after making the meal, but he'd begun the habit with their mother and felt it was important to pass that courtesy to his daughters as well. Seth had still not let go of her hand when her father finally came around to him in his natural order of serving the meal. It was always the women first, then any male guests. Seth knew the order since he'd eaten with them plenty of times. Still, he held fast to her hand until she squeezed it, causing him to nearly drop his plate as he held it out toward her father for a spoonful of scrambled eggs.

Ruthie bit her bottom lip to keep from giggling at Seth's clumsiness, her father unaware of what was going on beneath the table. She had a mind to test him further, but he finally let go of her hand to balance his plate to keep the eggs from rolling onto the table. Ruthie found the entire thing quite comical and hoped he wouldn't get aggravated with her antics and refuse her request for help with her pumpkins. His flat-bed wagon would be able to carry the entire batch she needed to take to the market. Whatever the reason he was not himself today, she thought it might be to her advantage if it had anything at all to do with her. She certainly hoped it was so.

Her father finished serving the eggs and bacon and then passed the plate of banana bread to Ruthie. After putting a slice on her plate, she turned to Seth to hand him the plate and her gaze met with his. She smiled and then watched his gaze travel to her lips; did he want to kiss her? Cousin Beth had told her that when a man wants to kiss you, they look at your lips to see how kissable they are. She wished they were alone so she could find out, but her father was sitting across the table from them. Albeit, he was busy shoveling eggs into his mouth, completely oblivious to what was going on right under his nose. Naomi was too busy daydreaming of marrying Jeremiah to notice either.

"It's banana-nut," Ruthie said, purposely breaking the spell between them so they wouldn't get caught doing *whatever* it was they were doing. "I made it fresh yesterday, but I warmed it up this morning."

He nodded nervously. *"Danki,"* he said, taking the plate from her and selecting a thick slice and putting it on his plate. "It's *mei* favorite."

"Mine too!" she said, smiling. "*Vadder* teases me that I could eat an entire loaf by myself—with a pound of butter!"

He chuckled, seemingly loosening up a little. "I think you might have to compete with me for it."

She flashed him a look that let him know she was up for the challenge and watched his cheeks turn a little pink. He lowered his head and started shoveling eggs into his mouth to cover it up, but Ruthie saw right through him. She thought it odd that he should react to her in such a strange way, but it was all happening so fast she wasn't certain how to process it. It was as if they'd noticed each other for the first time—in a way they would not have normally thought. At least it was that way for her. She had no way of knowing what he was thinking, and she wasn't about to ask him; seeing his cheeks heat up was more exciting—as if they shared some unspoken secret between them. What exactly that secret was, she had no idea, but she was willing to bet it was going to be fun finding out.

Within minutes, her father had gobbled up his plateful and was helping himself to seconds. Ruthie rose slightly from her chair, reaching over the table with the coffee pot to pour him a second cup, then she topped off Seth's cup without looking at him. She knew he would stay put at the table until he finished—only to be polite, and she would keep him there until after her father finished if she could help it. It was the only way to have a moment alone with him to ask the question that was burning in her.

"More eggs?" she offered Seth while she was still out of her chair.

He nodded politely, a mouthful of bread keeping him from speaking. Ruthie lifted the lid on the eggs and scooped a heaping serving spoonful and dropped it on his plate. Then she sifted through the paper towels for the last layer of bacon and put one piece on her own plate and two more on Seth's without asking. She'd left the last two strips for her father, and right on cue, he snatched them up before she could drop the paper towels back onto the plate. Meanwhile, she flashed a sideways glance at Naomi who was dreamily chomping on her first slice of bacon and still had enough on her plate that could last her another hour if she didn't pick up the pace.

"What time is Jeremiah expecting to pick you up this morning?" Ruthie asked her dreamy-eyed sister.

Naomi glanced up at the battery-operated clock on the kitchen wall, and her eyes bulged. "He'll be here any minute!" she stuffed the last few spoons-full of eggs in her mouth, picked up her plate and reached over and pecked her father on the cheek. Then she put the ends of the bacon strips in her mouth and let them hang while she picked up her dishes and carried them over to the sink.

Buggy wheels and horse's hooves alerted them that Jeremiah had arrived and Naomi excused herself to go up to her room to fetch her sweater. Ruthie knew she was going upstairs to brush her teeth so that she would have fresh breath to kiss Jeremiah, but she didn't tease her for it the way she had before when they were out of earshot of their father.

The back door received a quick knock and swung open, and Jeremiah entered the kitchen looking for Naomi. His gaze landed on Seth, and Ruthie hadn't missed the look of bewilderment in his eyes. The cousins had rivaled over Naomi, and she'd thought it was over, but the look of surprise at Seth's presence at the breakfast table let her know there was still a twinge of jealousy still lingering in Jeremiah.

"What brings you to breakfast this morning, Seth?" Jeremiah asked.

"Bales of hay," her father said without looking up from his plate. "*Gutemariye*, Jeremiah; I'd ask you to join us, but I'm afraid we finished before you arrived. There's plenty of *kaffi* if you'd like a cup."

Her father motioned to Ruthie to get another cup, but Jeremiah declined. "*Nee, danki,* but I have to drop Naomi off at the *haus,* and then I have to be at the lumber mill for my shift, or I'll be late."

Ruthie sat back down next to Seth, and she sensed the tension between the two cousins, and she worried a fight might break out between them the way he'd recently fought with Silas over Annie.

"What about you, Seth?" Jeremiah asked, his jaw clenching. "I thought you told me you had a full day of delivering to do? When I rode by, it looked like you'd barely made a dent in your field."

"He's helping *me* today with *mei* pumpkins!" Ruthie burst out without thinking. "I don't have any way to get them to market today without making several trips, and he offered the use of his flat-bed wagon."

Seth looked at her, paused, and then nodded with a smile. "*Jah*, I promised Ruthie I'd help her with the pumpkins."

Giddiness rose in Ruthie at her small victory, but she suspected there might be some reluctance in Seth. It didn't matter; he'd promised in front of her father and Jeremiah, so he would help her whether he wanted to or not. She hadn't meant to put him on the spot, but she thought it might divert Jeremiah's agitation with his cousin if he believed Seth's presence there this morning was for Ruthie and not Naomi. She saw the opportunity, and she took it; she needed his help, and she could see that asking him in private might have given him the chance to tell her he wasn't able to. This way, she got what she wanted, and there would be peace between the cousins.

Ruthie told herself it was all for the best, but she suspected that Seth's helping her would put him behind in his work. She suddenly felt bad for putting him on the spot, but as soon as they finished the meal, she would give him the chance to back out of his promise. At least she would offer, knowing he wouldn't take it, and hoped that would ease her conscience. It wasn't that she didn't care, but she also felt a sudden intrigue about his strange reactions to her during the meal. He'd held her hand as if he was thinking of dating her. Was it possible he'd ask her for a buggy ride before they finished taking the pumpkins into town?

Would she tell him yes if he asked her? Her knee-jerk reaction would be yes, but would it only be because she was still angry with Jacob for going away on *rumspringa* without her? No, Jacob had proven himself to be irresponsible and immature; he was certainly not the marrying type. Was Seth?

Naomi came downstairs with her sweater, and when she walked by, Ruthie could smell the minty-fresh mouthwash she used. She giggled inwardly at her sister and wondered if she should use some of the mouthwash before she went out to the pumpkin patch with Seth—just in case.

After her sister and Jeremiah left the house, her father rose from his chair and pushed it under the table. He looked at Seth, who was still eating. "I'll see you later," he said. "*Danki* for the hay—and for helping Ruthie with the pumpkins."

When he was out the back door, Ruthie got up from the table and began stacking the empty plates and utensils. She looked up at Seth, who seemed engrossed in his meal.

"You don't have to help me," she offered. "I was only trying to put Jeremiah's mind at ease and let him know you weren't running after Naomi. I didn't want *mei schweschder* to have trouble with him; she's suffered through enough worry."

He looked up from his plate and set his fork down. "I can appreciate that—and I don't mind helping you," he said, his cheeks pinking up again. "I want you to know that I realized I didn't like your *schweschder* that way; *mei* cousin knows that, but he has always been jealous of *mei* friendship with Naomi. But now that she is getting married, our childhood friendship has to end. It is the proper way."

"*Jah,* I suspect your cousin feels the same way about your friendship with Naomi."

He emptied his coffee cup and patted his stomach. "I'm afraid if I finish that second helping you piled on me I'll be rolling around the pumpkin patch with your pumpkins."

Ruthie giggled. "I'm sorry; I wanted to give you enough food to make you stay after *mei dat* and Naomi left so I could *ask* you about helping me with the pumpkins."

He smiled when she grabbed his plate but snatched the remainder of his banana bread from it. "I still have enough room for this," he said, popping it into his mouth.

CHAPTER THREE

Seth followed Ruthie out to her pumpkin patch feeling his belly was so full it was making him sluggish. He'd been up for three hours already making deliveries to the local farms after loading his wagon in the dark. The Yoder place had been his last stop before heading back home to load up again and make more deliveries, except that the very savvy Ruthie had volunteered him to help get her pumpkins into town so she could sell them at the market. He thought it was cute the way she'd tricked him into helping her—clever even, and though he didn't have time to help her, he wasn't going to back out. Not only was it the neighborly thing to do, but she'd held onto his hand for so long under the table, he had to wonder if she liked him. He'd never really given Ruthie much thought, but he supposed she was already thinking about marriage since her birthday; that, and the fact her sister would be marrying in only a couple of weeks. Most of the young women in the community suffered from *wedding fever* this time of year, each hoping to get a proposal. He supposed Ruthie was no different from the rest of her peers.

He looked around, feeling a little overwhelmed; she hadn't even begun to pick the pumpkins yet. It would take hours to gather them with the wheel barrow he'd brought with them and transfer them to his flat-bed wagon; it would take another hour at least, to get them to town and unloaded. What had he been thinking when he allowed her to trick him into helping her? The truth was, he hadn't been thinking about anything except the warmth of her hand that sent a spark of gooseflesh all the way up his arm when she'd held fast to it under the table at breakfast. He'd never experienced such a charge of excitement from a female, and he'd dated his fair share of young women in the community. None had made him unable to think straight with a mere touch the way Ruthie had. Was it possible he could develop feelings for her that quickly? One thing was certain; they were going to spend an awfully long time together today, and that would give him plenty of time to figure it out—wouldn't it?

He watched her skip through to the middle of the oversized pumpkin patch. He could see that she'd planted pie-pumpkins as well as decorative gourds. He only knew that much about them because his mother had planted a few of each in her garden over the years. But now, it seemed, he was taking an interest in Ruthie's overly-large pumpkin patch.

"Where do you want me to begin?" he asked, looking around at all the ripe pumpkins. He loved their rich amber hue that reminded him of the maple leaves this time of year. They paled in comparison to the sweet aroma the maple leaves cast as the trees shed them in preparation for the onset of winter. A warm breeze ruffled the large leaves on the vines, and he chuckled at the sound.

"I've never been in a pumpkin patch this large before," he said. "It sounds as if the leaves are clapping!"

Ruthie paused to listen and then let out a giggle. "I never thought about it before, but you're right."

She stopped in the middle of the field and turned toward the road. "I'd like to leave that for the harvest festival in town next week because that's where my prize-pumpkin is." She pointed to the large, orange and cream-colored pumpkin near the front of the patch but Seth had already noticed it when he walked past it. "I'm going to enter it into the *Most Unique Pumpkin* contest; it has unusual markings on it—as if it somehow got crossed with a gourd."

"I've never seen a marbled pumpkin before," Seth said. "It's the most unusual pumpkin I've ever seen; I'm sure that one will win."

Ruthie clucked her tongue. "Maybe; don't you remember last year a man had a pumpkin in the shape of a heart?"

"*Jah,* but I bet he couldn't grow another one if he tried!" Seth said. "Besides, that pumpkin you've got is the only one of its kind that I've seen."

Ruthie sighed. "*Danki,* but I wish I had one big enough to enter into the *Largest Pumpkin* category, but I didn't get one that big this year."

"I'm sure you've got a prize-winner with your marble pumpkin; I'd sure vote for it."

Ruthie giggled. "Then I wish you were one of the judges!"

"What is the prize?"

"One Hundred Dollars!" she gushed. "That money would be a big help."

"That would be a big help," he agreed. "Are you entering anything else?"

She nodded. "My pumpkin whoopie pies with the secret ingredient in the filling!"

"Those are sure to win!" he said. "I've never tasted anything like them."

She giggled. "That's because of the secret ingredient."

"I hope you come home with two first prizes," he said.

"Danki," she said with a smile that made his heart sing. "Let's start with this row. I can cut them if you load them onto the wheel barrow."

An hour later, Seth felt his legs wobble a little from the many trips he'd made back and forth from the edge of the pumpkin patch to the road where he'd parked his horse and his wagon. He'd already put in a full day of work, and his arms ached from toting the wheel barrow back and forth so many times. He wasn't about to complain; in that hour, he'd almost worked up enough nerve to ask Ruthie to take a buggy ride with him. They were getting along so magically he was certain he'd get a yes from her on the way home from town.

When they'd loaded the last batch, he upturned the wheel barrow and loaded it onto the end of the wagon and then helped Ruthie up into the seat. He took her back around to her driveway so she could fetch her baked goods for the market.

Once they were on their way into town, Seth found it tough to concentrate with Ruthie sitting so close to him. She chattered on about the contest and how excited she was that she could potentially bring home Two Hundred Dollars in prizes. He planned to ask her to be his date for the harvest festival next Saturday, but only if she gave a favorable answer to taking a buggy ride with him. He couldn't help but think that in some ways, they were taking their first buggy ride now. Though it didn't count because this was more of a favor, and she'd been the one to do the asking. He aimed to change that just as soon as they were on the way home from the market.

Ruthie hopped down from Seth's wagon thinking how warm it had been on the small bench sitting so close to him. Their knees had knocked together practically the entire way, and it almost seemed as if Seth was trying to get her attention. She giggled inwardly thinking it was a little bit appealing and she wondered if she was going to get an invitation to take a buggy ride with him in the near future.

She walked around to the back of the wagon to start unloading the pumpkins as she looked for Mr. Murdock but didn't see him. Under the tented area near the cash register, Ruthie spotted a young man—a few years older than she was—twenty-one, perhaps. His tight, white t-shirt carried the Murdock's Circle-B logo on the sleeve and conformed to his trim physique. She could easily see the contours of his chest and the ripples of his abs where the shirt hung over the narrow waist of his jeans that hugged him all over—not that she was looking that closely! His hair swished to one side just over his eyebrows and amazingly stayed in place. She guessed he used hairspray. She liked the unkempt look that made him seem almost rebellious. She'd never seen him there before and wondered if he might be a new employee.

Seth followed her gaze to the young man and then flashed her a sideways glance. "I thought you said an old man ran this market."

Ruthie shrugged, pulling her gaze from the handsome *Englisher. "Jah,* Mr. Murdock; he told me he'd be here this morning to meet me. Maybe he'll be here before we finish unloading all the pumpkins. It's only nine o'clock."

Seth busied himself unloading the pumpkins while Ruthie reached under the seat of the buckboard for her container of baked-goods. From behind her, a warm pair of hands reached for the box, his touch sending tingles up her arm.

"Let me help you with that," his smoky baritone voice making the hair at the nape of her neck prickling.

She turned around while he was reaching and found herself practically in his arms. He didn't move, and neither did she; the gleam in his blue eyes making her heart thump. He smiled slowly, and she could feel heat rising in her cheeks.

"Where do you want these, Ruthie?" The annoyance in Seth's tone broke the spell between her and the man standing dangerously close to her.

She straightened and lowered her gaze while he backed away. Flipping his head to the side with a short, controlled shake, his hair feathered back into place across his forehead.

He pointed to an empty table under the canopy. "You can put them there." Then he turned to Ruthie. "I'm Chad Murdock. My grandfather broke his leg a few days ago, so he won't be able to work for the rest of the season. He told me he was expecting you today; you must be Ruthie Yoder."

His smile nearly melted her into a puddle. *"Jah,* I am Ruthie; it's nice to meet you, Chad. I'm sorry about your grandfather; I will keep him in my prayers."

"That's very kind of you," he said.

"We arranged for the baked-goods on a trial-basis, so it's up to him if he wants to let me bring more. I can bring one more batch of pumpkins next Saturday before the harvest festival begins."

Chad nodded. "That sounds good; we don't grow pumpkins since they take up so much space, so we're grateful for what you can bring for us to sell. He gave me your paperwork; I can go over it if you'd like me to."

Seth looked up from the second batch of pumpkins he'd loaded since she'd begun talking to Chad. "I have to get back to my deliveries, Ruthie; didn't you already discuss the pay-rate with his grandfather?"

Ruthie's face heated. *"Jah,* I did, but *danki* for asking."

She glanced up at Seth when he tossed the wheel barrow up onto the bed of the wagon with a thud, a look of impatience clouding his handsome face.

Did he just roll his eyes at me?

Her heart pounded heavily against her ribs; the last thing she wanted to do was make him angry—or was it jealousy she sensed in him?

CHAPTER FOUR

Robin Baker pushed out her bottom lip, showing her best pouty-face. "I thought you said you could get your grandpa to sell *my* baked goods at your farmer's market," she said in a whiny voice.

Chad tried to shrug her away; she was being clingy and whiny, and he didn't like it when she did that. "I told you I'd ask him, but he already contracted this Amish girl's stuff. I could always tell her I can't take any more orders until my grandfather gets back. The old man won't be back this season, but she doesn't have to know that."

She smiled wickedly. "That's the smartest thing you've said all morning!"

He took a bite of Ruthie's pumpkin bread and closed his eyes, moaning at the taste.

Robin nudged him. "Hey! You never make noises like that when you eat the stuff I bake."

He licked his fingers after setting the half-eaten slice of bread down on the paper plate. "That's because you never made pumpkin bread like this before. You should try it—it melts in your mouth!"

"I don't want to try it," she complained, folding her arms over her narrow waist and pouting. "She probably uses dirty, brown eggs from her chickens and milk from her dirty old cow!"

"What makes you think her farm animals are so dirty?" Chad asked, annoyance apparent in his tone.

"Amish people don't use electricity, and I doubt they have indoor plumbing," Robin said with a mean smirk. "I'll bet she hasn't had a bath in a month!"

"What do her bathing habits have to do with how clean her farm animals are?" he asked. "From what I hear, Amish people are hard workers, and I'll bet they take really good care of their animals. Have you ever driven by an Amish farm? Their barns are always freshly-painted, and there's clean wash on their clotheslines every Monday!"

Robin scrunched up her nose. "Since when are you such an expert on the Amish?"

"I'm not, but my grandfather speaks very highly of them."

"Just don't let that girl fool you with her Amish charm," Robin warned.

She snatched the last bite of bread from his plate and shoved it in her mouth. She cinched her brow and tipped her head to the side while she chewed; she was thinking, and Chad didn't like the devious look in her eyes.

When she finished, her eyes grew wide. "You *have* to get me this recipe! Do you have any idea how much money this bread could bring in for my bakery?"

Chad scrunched up his face. "Isn't there some law against using someone else's recipes or something?"

She guffawed. "Not if they *give* it to you willingly. I'm betting you can talk the little Amish girl into giving you her recipe. I saw the way she was mooning over you!"

Chad clucked his tongue. "She wasn't mooning."

"I was standing on the corner waiting for the light to change and I got a good look at her face," Robin said. "She certainly had stars in her eyes for you."

Chad puffed up his chest and jutted out his chin. "Who could blame her?"

Robin looped her arm in his and gave it a squeeze. "Just make sure that little crush is only one-sided."

"I'm insulted that you think I like that girl; she's way too young."

Robin laughed. "Not just way too young—she's way too Amish!"

"Amish or not, I don't like her."

Robin kissed his cheek. "I'm glad to hear that. I wouldn't have to fight for you."

"I didn't think you liked me for anything more than what I can do for you!" he said.

She smiled and put a finger under his chin. "Your looks are the only thing tempting me, but you and I are too much alike, and that's a dangerous combination. I'm afraid you might get full of yourself one of these days and think you can overpower me. Keep your relationship with the Amish girl to a minimum; I wouldn't want that getting in my way."

Chad cut another slice of Ruthie's pumpkin bread and put it on his plate. "You don't have to worry about my *relationship* with her. The only competition you have to worry about with her is this bread."

Robin picked it up from the plate. "Not if you get me the recipe!"

"I thought you could tell any ingredient just by the taste," he said. "Can't you just guess what's in it?"

She took another bite and chewed it slowly, shaking her head. "No; she put something in it that I can't figure out—like a secret ingredient. There's something about the taste of it I can't figure out."

Chad picked up one of the pie-pumpkins Ruthie had left with him. "Maybe it's her pumpkins; she grows them herself. She probably uses manure from her *dirty* cows to fertilize them!"

Robin spat out the piece of bread onto the ground and growled at him while he threw his head back and laughed.

Red-faced, Robin threw the remaining slice of bread at him. "That's not funny!"

Chad couldn't stop laughing—especially when she picked up a wrapped loaf of the bread and stormed off with it toward her bakery around the corner.

Seth fidgeted in the lull of conversation that had fallen between him and Ruthie. Up until now, he'd had to listen to non-stop praise of *Chad,* and what a great guy he is for helping his grandfather, *blah blah blah.* He didn't dislike the guy, but he wasn't as enthusiastic about him as Ruthie was. He was nearing her farm, and he hadn't even gotten up the nerve to ask her for a buggy ride yet.

"Would you like a ride into town on Monday when you go to the market to settle up with them?" he asked, his voice a little shaky. "I have to go to the lumber yard to pick up supplies to fix my chicken coop."

It wasn't exactly an invitation, but it would give him a chance to spend more time with her. That, and to keep an eye on that smooth-talking Chad.

She smiled. "*Danki,* it will save my poor feet the pain from walking there and back."

Seth straightened up in his seat, a bit more confident of his chances with Ruthie. "If you'd like, we can have lunch together at the deli afterward," he suggested.

"I'll have to time my washing just right on Monday to make certain I've got a load on the line before we go."

"Since I'm driving you back and forth, we could use the extra time it would have taken you to walk to get some lunch," he said matter-of-factly.

She giggled. "That is true."

He slapped at the reins to move his gelding up her driveway. "It's settled then."

He almost wished tomorrow was a church week so he could take her home from the service, which was a sure sign they were officially courting, but it hadn't even dawned on him last Sunday. It amused him how determined he was to court her in the short time he'd spent with her today, yet he'd never considered her up until now. Sure, she'd always been the one who laughed at his jokes, and he certainly cared enough about her to help her in any way, but today was somehow different. He supposed it was because today was the first time he'd noticed what a beautiful young woman she'd grown up to be.

He stopped the buggy just outside her kitchen door, and she hopped out and turned to smile at him. "See you on Monday—about eleven o'clock?'

He nodded, returning the smile, his heart doing somersaults behind his ribs.

Robin turned the key in the back door of *The Baker's Dozen* from the alley, breathing in the aroma of pumpkin pie.

Her aunt Rita looked up at her and frowned. "You took your time with that bank deposit. I was beginning to worry you'd gotten mugged."

She clucked her tongue. "Do you really think I'd let someone steal shopping money from me?"

Her aunt laughed, not looking up from the tray of jack-o-lantern cookies she was sprinkling sugar over. "Probably not; what took you so long then? They have a sale on shoes at *The Hat Box?*"

"Ew! I wouldn't shop there; that place is for old people!"

Rita looked up and scowled. "I happen to like that place!"

Robin snickered. "Which is *why I don't!*"

"Then where have you been for the last hour while I managed to bake all the pies for today's orders?"

Robin let out a loud sigh. "I stopped by the farmer's market to see Chad; he's filling in for his grandfather. He broke a hip or something," she said, her tone snotty.

"What do you have there?" Rita asked, eyeing the loaf of pumpkin bread.

"Just some pumpkin bread an Amish girl made; Chad is selling it for her at the farmer's market. I was hoping you could tell me what her secret ingredient is so I can make some. I'd like to enter it into the bake-off at the harvest festival next Saturday."

"Resorting to using someone else's recipes?" Rita asked. "That must be some bread."

"I'll admit it's really good," Robin said, her tone dripping with jealousy. "That's why you *have* to help me figure out what's in it. We could make a fortune selling this stuff. We could advertise it as being from an old Amish recipe."

Rita set down the sifter in the sugar bowl and looked at her niece. "That's stooping kind of low, even for you, Robin!"

"Look, Aunt Rita; Daddy put *me* in charge here," she said. "This was my birthday present."

Rita held her hands up and forced a smile. "I know; I'm only the hired help!"

Robin put on her pouty-face. "I didn't mean it like that; please say you'll help me."

She knew her aunt couldn't say no to her when she pouted.

"You look just like your mother when you do that; she used to use that face to get anything she wanted from me, so don't you start in on me."

"Yes, Ma'am," Robin said, mocking her aunt.

Rita reached for the pumpkin bread and unwrapped it, bringing it close to her face and breathing it in. "It smells scrumptious!"

Robin rolled her eyes. "Unfortunately, it tastes even better than it smells!"

Her aunt broke a chunk off the end and took a bite, her eyes rolling closed and her head tipping back as she moaned from the taste.

Robin planted her fists on her hips and sighed. "I wish I could get that kind of reaction from *my* baking. Now you know why I want this recipe so badly."

"Mm-hm," Rita said, her eyes still closed as she finished chewing. "Oh-my-gosh, that has got to be the *best* pumpkin bread I've ever tasted."

"See? What did I tell you?"

She took another bite. "Oh," she said, her mouth full. "I can't get enough of this—it's heavenly!"

Robin blew out a loud breath, "I wouldn't go *that* far!"

"I would," Rita said, stuffing another bite in her mouth.

"Okay; you've had enough!" Robin said angrily. "Tell me what's in it."

Rita continued to chew. "You mean, besides a little piece of Heaven?"

Robin stomped her foot like a child. "I'm serious."

Rita's eyes bulged. "So am I; forget the recipe; I think you need to find that girl and hire her."

"I don't need to hire her; I *need* her recipes!"

"I think you'd be better off if you hired her," Rita said.

Robin slapped her hand on the stainless-steel work station. "I don't want advice; I want the ingredients. Can you figure out what it is?"

"If I had to guess, I'd say she used real butter—not the kind you get in the store—but the farm-fresh kind. And eggs right out from under the hens!"

"Gross!" Robin said.

"You asked," Rita said with a chuckle. "But you're right; there is something else— another ingredient, and I can't put my finger on it. I'm sorry, kiddo."

Robin let out a loud sigh that almost came out like a low growl.

"I'll get that recipe even if I have to make friends with that Amish girl."

Rita laughed. "I can't wait to see that!"

CHAPTER FIVE

Seth had practically begged his mother to let him drive her over to the Yoder's to drop off the pie she'd baked. She'd been widowed for more than five years now, and though he suspected his mother was looking for an invite to take supper with the Widower Yoder, he didn't dare say so. Besides, he was hoping if he tagged along, he'd get an invite too. After all, he'd practically had to sit on his hands to keep from going over there on his own; at least his mother's pie was a far better excuse than he could have come up with on his own. He'd been eager to see Ruthie, and he probably would have drummed up an excuse on his own sooner or later, but the day was wearing on. Using his mother's eagerness to visit with the widower took the burden off him since there was no way he was going to be able to wait until tomorrow afternoon to see her.

When they pulled into the driveway of the Yoder farm, Ruthie was sitting on the porch shelling peas. She raised a hand to wave as they pulled forward, and Seth couldn't help but return her warm smile and friendly wave. His heart sped up, confirming his anticipation in seeing her. Was he falling for her? It seemed a little sudden, but his cousin had warned him that when it was the right girl, the love can sneak up on you. He clenched his jaw, hoping to keep his mother from noticing he was smiling but it was too late. He could see from the gleam in her eye she hadn't missed it.

"It seems Ruthie is a little sweet on you," his mother said.

He shook his head, keeping his jaw steady. "*Nee,* I don't think so," he said, keeping his head down to hide embarrassment.

"I think she'd make a *gut fraa,*" she said.

Seth parked the closed buggy and ran around the other side to help his mother out, but Mr. Yoder was already there.

Where had he come from? Had the widower heard what his mother had said to him? He prayed not, but he hadn't even noticed him when he'd pulled the buggy beside the barn. Seth stood back and watched the expression on the older man's face go from worried to almost a boyish gleam—the same dreamy-eyed look his mother got in her eyes every time she brought him up. Was it possible they were courting right under Seth's nose? And if so, for how long?

He watched his mother and the widower walk into the house without a word to him. Dumfounded, he walked around to the front of the house and climbed the steps in a stupor.

"What's wrong, Seth?"

He looked up, not realizing Ruthie had said something to him. "What did you say?"

She moved the colander of shelled peas closer to her and beckoned him to sit on the swing with her. "You look sort of strange; are you alright?"

"*Jah,*" he said, collapsing onto the swing and jostling it almost enough to make Ruthie drop the colander. "*Ach,* I'm sorry." He grabbed for the colander, covering his hands over hers, a spark of energy traveling up his arm.

Is that going to happen every time I'm near her?

"Did you notice anything strange about your *dat* and *mei mamm?*"

She shrugged. "How do you mean?"

He pulled in a breath, wondering how to put his worries into words. "Do you think they're *courting?*"

It wasn't the most tactful thing to say, but there was no other way to put it. From the look on her face, she wasn't shocked in the least.

She lifted the corners of her mouth into a smile, her eyes gleaming. "Isn't it wonderful for them if they are? I mean, I've wondered the same thing, but you have to admit; the signs are all there."

Seth picked up a handful of shelled peas and shoved them in his mouth. "I suppose it is, but don't you think that would be a little odd—I mean, for our parents to marry—if they do?"

"I suppose she'll be moving in here," Ruthie said with excitement. "It would be nice to have a *mamm* again."

He supposed for a young woman, having a mother was important; for him, having a father was something he dearly missed, but he doubted the Widower Yoder could ever measure up—no matter how close they'd become in the years since his father had passed away.

He wondered how that would affect the relationship between him and Ruthie—if they should marry. His mother would be her step-mother and her mother-in-law. It would be something to get used to, but perhaps if he proposed before Ruthie's father did it wouldn't be that bad. Was he ready for that yet? It seemed that her father had a head start on him; at least they were courting. He hadn't even worked up the nerve to ask Ruthie for a buggy ride yet. Had his mother and the widower had a buggy ride already? Surely, he would have heard something about it; or perhaps the older folks did things a little differently than the youth.

"You know," she said quietly. "If they do marry and your *mudder* moves in here, you'll have your *haus* all to yourself; I've always wondered what that would feel like."

I would have room to have a familye of mei own, he thought.

"I suppose it would be lonely to live all by yourself—unless I had a *familye* of my own," he said, hoping she'd take a hint.

She sighed whimsically. "*Jah,* but if you lived alone, you could do anything you wanted—without anyone telling you what to do."

Seth chuckled. "Maybe not any humans, but the animals would sure make a ruckus if I didn't feed them on time—or let them out of the barn. My clothes would always be dirty, and I'd starve if I didn't fix myself a meal."

She sighed again, this time, disappointment seemed to weigh it down. "I suppose I never thought of it that way."

"You wouldn't want to live alone, would you?" he asked.

"I used to think so—until *mamm* died," she admitted. "But then I realized that no matter how much my older sister might annoy me, I'm going to miss her once she's married to your cousin."

Seth's mother poked her head out the screen door and smiled. "Your *vadder* invited us to eat with you; I hope you don't mind, Ruthie, but I took the roast out of the oven."

Ruthie jumped up from the swing. "*Danki.*" She looked down at the colander in her hands. "*Ach,* I forgot to steam the peas."

Seth grabbed a handful and smiled at her. "That's okay; I prefer them fresh."

She giggled. "Me too!"

Ruthie was hanging up the last pair of her father's broadfall pants on the clothesline when Seth pulled his open buggy into the yard.

If anyone sees us in the open buggy, they will think we are courting!

Her heart fluttered at the thought of it and wondered if it was purposeful on Seth's part. He hadn't officially asked her yet, but perhaps this was his gentle way of easing her into the idea. Surely, he knew what others would think; was he hoping they would? On top of that, he was early, and she'd wanted to have time to change into a more suitable dress for town instead of her brown work dress.

Embarrassed by her appearance, she held up a hand to him before he had a chance to jump down from the seat. "I'll only be a minute," she said with a raised voice as she hurried toward the kitchen door. "*Mei* dress is wet, and I need a dry one."

"It'll dry on the way into town," Seth said with a chuckle.

She didn't find any humor in his statement, so she simply ignored him and continued into the house. She washed and dressed quickly and was back out the kitchen door to avoid making him wait.

His expression stopped her from approaching his buggy. "You look like you're on your way to your *wedding!*"

She looked down at the skirt of her blue dress and the organdy apron and then touched the organdy prayer *kapp* she'd slipped on after smoothing back her hair into the neat bun it was when she'd begun her chores that morning.

Realizing she must look a little like a bride, she made an excuse. "It was *mei* only clean dress," she said. It wasn't a lie, but she hadn't intentionally wanted to look like she was fishing for a proposal either. Would the rumors fly if she was seen in Seth's courting buggy wearing her Sunday best dress on a Monday?

"*Ach,* I forgot today was wash day," he said with a smile. "But you know tongues are going to wag if someone sees us."

Ruthie blushed. "Are you alright with that? If not; I can change back into *mei* work dress,"

He chuckled as he hopped down to assist her into his buggy. "Let them talk!"

Ruthie smiled and took his hand, his warm touch sending tingles all the way up her elbow.

Once she was seated next to him, he set the horse moving toward the main road, and when he turned, he tucked his arm behind her on the back of the seat. She leaned into his arm, feeling the same warm tingling.

Did she like him that way? She'd never felt that way when she'd ridden home with a couple of the youth after an occasional singing, but she hadn't been serious about any of them, and so she'd not accepted more than one ride from any of them.

She pondered her curiosity as she gazed over her shoulder at the neighboring farms, their wash flapping in the warm breeze on their clotheslines. She almost felt disappointed that no one was out in their yards or on their porches to see her riding by with Seth. Would she be embarrassed if they did?

She trained her eyes on him; his chiseled jawline peppered with stubble that matched his dark blonde hair.

"You can drop me off at the farmer's market, and I'll walk up the block to meet you when I finish," Ruthie said.

"Nee, what kind of a *mann* would I be if I left you alone with Chad?"

Ruthie narrowed her eyes. "What's wrong with chad?"

"I don't trust him," Seth said. "You need to be careful around the *Englishers.*"

"I spend plenty of time around *Englishers;* you are almost acting like you're *jealous.*"

Seth steered the horse into the square and around the corner to the farmer's market. "I'm not jealous; I just don't want him to take advantage of you. *Englishers* treat us like we're *dummkopfs.*"

"I'm sure Chad isn't like that," Ruthie defended him. "His grandfather is a *gut mann,* so he comes from humble stock. The apple doesn't fall far from the tree."

Seth chuckled. "Just be careful; we both know rotten apples can fall from *gut* trees!"

If this was Seth being jealous, she wasn't sure how she felt about it. In some ways it was cute, and it certainly let her know that he was interested, but in others, she wondered if he wasn't letting his jealousy cloud his judgment of Chad.

He drove his buggy up to the curb in front of the farmer's market, and before he could hop down to the other side to help Ruthie down from the seat, Chad was there with his hand out to her.

She smiled shyly, her face heating. "*Danki,*"

Chad tucked her arm in his, and the two walked away from the buggy without so much as a *goodbye* or *thank you* to Seth. What was it about this *Englisher* that intrigued her so? He was certainly nice to look at, but his charm and mannerisms were very controlled and bold while maintaining a gentleman quality. Perhaps Seth had been wrong about him. She turned, realizing too late that she'd forgotten about him; he'd already pulled away from the curb and was heading down the road.

"I was hoping we could have a few moments to ourselves," Chad said. "I don't think your brother likes me."

Her heart thumped wildly. Chad thinks Seth is *mei brudder?*

"*Ach,* he's not…"

"You'll be happy to know," Chad said, interrupting her. "That I sold every one of your loaves of pumpkin bread and most of your pumpkins."

She giggled. "That's *gut* news, *jah?*"

When they approached the canopied area, Chad let her arm slip from his, and her arm tingled a little, though not the way her hand had when Seth had helped her into his buggy before the trip. Nor did his touch stir the butterflies in her stomach the same as having Seth's arm around the back of the open buggy on the ride over. Although she couldn't deny Chad was handsome and exciting, if she had to compare; Seth stirred feelings in her that made her wish he'd ask her for an official buggy ride. After a pleasant supper with him last night, she thought for sure and for certain the invitation would come but it didn't.

Perhaps if Seth becomes jealous enough, he'll get around to it!

CHAPTER SIX

Seth pulled his buggy up to the curb in front of the farmer's market and looked for Ruthie, a twinge of jealousy pulling at his heartstrings when he spotted her getting cozy with Chad. Ruthie was laughing at whatever it was he was saying, while Chad leaned against a big oak tree and flirted shamelessly with her. It annoyed Seth, but what could he do about it? He had no claim on her, no matter how much he might wish for it. So he sat there in his buggy and waited, wondering if he should jump down and get her.

Nee, if he's asking her out for a date, I would only make a fool of myself. I wish I could have gotten up the nerve to ask her for that buggy ride on the way over here; then she'd be spoken-for and I'd have nothing to worry about with Chad.

Changing his mind, Seth jumped down and walked around his buggy, pretending to check the harnesses and his gelding's shoes. He looked up intermittently, hoping Ruthie would notice he was there, but she was too engrossed in her conversation with Chad.

Ruthie took the money from Chad, aware that Seth had been waiting for a few minutes, and she didn't want to make him wait. Though she had enjoyed listening to Chad's stories about life on his grandfather's farm, she had a lunch date with Seth, and she was looking forward to it.

"I can't believe all my pumpkin bread sold out in the first hour!" she said, putting the envelope of money in her apron pocket.

"It's the most delicious pumpkin bread I've ever tasted."

Ruthie raised her eyebrows. "You tried it?"

"I bought one for myself," Chad said. "And another one to take home to my mother."

"You didn't have to buy them; I would have given them to you."

Chad shook his head. "Nonsense! I'm a paying customer just like all the others. But I would like to ask a favor—for my mother."

Ruthie tucked flyaway hair behind her prayer *kapp* to keep it from slapping at her face in the breeze. "You want a favor from me for your *mudder?"*

Chad nodded. "She loved your bread so much she made me promise to ask you if she could have the recipe."

The request caught her off-guard, but she didn't see any reason not to give it to him. No one had ever asked her for a recipe before. *"Jah,* I can write it down for you if you have a piece of paper."

"Thank you!" Chad said, wasting no time in getting her a sheet of paper and a pen. "My mother will be so happy to have this."

Ruthie smiled. "You have to promise me something," she said as she began to write ingredients on the page.

Chad nodded before she finished. "Anything you say!"

"You have to let me know how it turns out—when your *mudder* makes it."

He continued to nod, now with more vigor. "Of course I will."

She finished quickly and bid him goodbye, and then skipped toward Seth, who was being all-too-obvious that he'd been watching her with Chad. It made her feel giddy that he was interested in her, but she sure hoped he would get around to asking her for a buggy ride—and soon.

Seth smiled as Ruthie approached, trying his best to keep his mouth shut about the chumminess between her and Chad. "Are you ready for some lunch?"

She nodded. "I'm starving!"

He patted his gelding. "I think I'll leave the buggy here since I already fed the meter."

"Jah, the deli is only down the next block, and it's a *gut* day for a walk."

He held out his arm, and she tucked her hand in the crook of his elbow. His gaze flickered toward Chad as they began their short excursion to the deli—just to make certain he was watching; he was. Though he knew the decision was up to Ruthie, Seth was determined to win her heart if he could.

"May I ask what it is you were writing for him?" he asked. The curiosity was killing him. "He wasn't making you sign something was he?"

"Nee, he asked me for the recipe for my pumpkin bread."

Seth stopped in front of the deli and whirled around to face her, his arm unlooping from hers. "And you gave it to him?" he asked with a raised voice.

Ruthie arched her eyebrows. "Why shouldn't I give it to him? It was for his *mudder.*"

"*Ach,* is that what he told you?"

Her nostrils flared. "I have no reason to doubt Chad; why would you?"

Seth paused; he knew if he didn't choose his words wisely, he was going to end up making Chad out to be a hero and himself as a cad for pointing out the obvious to her.

"Let me ask you this; did he order anymore bread from you?"

"*Nee,*" she answered slowly. "But he said he has to wait and get his grandfather's permission. It's not his market to say one way or the other; Mr. Murdock makes the decisions—not Chad."

"*Ach,* you don't think even for a minute that he wanted the recipe so he could make the bread himself and cut you out of the profits?"

"Nee, he said it was for his *mudder,* and I believe him."

Seth threw his hands up; he knew when he was defeated. Only time would tell if Chad was telling the truth or not, and he aimed to find out. He let the matter drop, knowing if he didn't it would ruin their lunch together and he was hoping to transition it into a date with her. Holding the door for her, he followed her into the deli, the aroma of freshly-baked bread and tomato-basil soup making his mouth water.

They went up to the counter and looked over the menu as they waited for the older couple in front of them to place their order.

Ruthie moved up once they finished. "I'll have the chicken and wild rice soup and half a corned beef sandwich on rye bread with Munster cheese, and a side of honey mustard."

"For your side salad?" the girl behind the counter asked with a bored tone.

"Caesar with extra parmesan cheese, please."

"And to drink?"

"Bottled water, please."

She punched in Ruthie's order and turned to Seth. "For you, Sir?"

"I'd like roast beef on wheat with Swiss cheese, Caesar salad with extra parmesan cheese, a cup of tomato-basil soup, and I'll have bottled water, too, please."

She punched his order into her computer and told him the total. She took his money and slid two bottles of water and a table number across the counter toward them and said, "*Next in line*," without even looking at them.

Seth followed Ruthie to a table in the corner and sat across from her. He gave her one of the bottled waters and opened his, taking a sip. "Bottled water?"

She giggled. "I like to spoil myself when I come into town," she said. "I hope you don't mind."

He nodded. "It's smoother than the well water," he commented.

"*Jah,* because there is a lot of rust in our water; I would drink it all the time, but *mei dat* would accuse me of trying to be too much like the *Englishers.*"

Seth couldn't imagine Ruthie as an *Englisher,* but he was willing to bet Chad had thought about it.

"There's nothing wrong with wanting filtered water," he said.

She smiled. "I would drink it every day if I could get away with it."

"I'm feeling a little spoiled too, right now," Seth said, smiling at her.

The girl from the front counter brought their food over and put it down in front of them and snatched the plastic number from the edge of the table and then left without a word, despite the two of them thanking her.

Seth reached across the table for Ruthie's hands, and she placed them in his, sending tingles up his arm again. He bowed his head and began the prayer.

"Lord, please bless the bounty that is before us and protect us while we are away from our homes. Please bless the young woman who served us today and the hands that prepared our meal. Amen."

"Amen," Ruthie whispered.

He reluctantly let go of her hands, the growling from his empty stomach winning over his emotions for the moment.

Chad held back the piece of paper containing Ruthie's recipe. "How much is it worth to you?" he teased. "You told me you could make a lot of money from this bread; I think it's only fair that I get part of the profits."

Robin planted her fists on her hips. "Why should I cut you in?"

She grabbed for it but Chad was taller than she was by at least a foot and he held it up too high for her to reach.

"No share; no recipe!"

She opened her purse and pulled out her checkbook. "How much do you want?"

He smirked. "How much is it worth to you?"

Robin rolled her eyes. "If I'd thought it was going to be this much hassle, I would have asked her myself!"

"But you don't know her," he said with a chuckle. "That's why you *need* me. I had to do a *lot* of flirting with that Amish girl to get that recipe for you."

"Somehow, I find it hard to believe that it was such a chore for you," she said. "I saw the way she was looking at you—like you're something we both know you're not!"

He switched hands, holding the paper above his head and out of her reach.

"Talk like that is going to cost you double," he said.

She pursed her lips and narrowed her eyes. "Fine!" she screeched. "I'll give you a hundred dollars for it."

He lowered his arm a little to tease her, and she grabbed for it, but he raised it even higher. "Not so fast; you'll get that much if you win first prize at the bakeoff. I want more than that."

"I don't care so much about that prize money," she said. "It's the blue ribbon I need; getting a local blue ribbon will increase my customer interest."

He laughed. "Now that I know how much it's worth to you, my price just went up!"

She stomped her foot and started writing the check; when she got to the amount, she asked him again.

Chad tipped his head and smiled. "I think a thousand dollars ought to cover it."

Robin gritted her teeth and growled at him. "That's too much!"

He waved the recipe above her head and laughed. "Think of the blue ribbon you could win."

She scribbled in the amount and ripped the check from the book and held it out to him, her breath heaving. When he reached for it, she snatched it away and held out her other hand for the recipe. "Hand it over at the same time because I don't trust you!"

He frowned. "I'm disappointed in you, Robin; I thought you liked me!"

She rolled her eyes again. "Yeah, not so much anymore. Here's your money; give me my recipe."

They exchanged the money and the recipe at the same time, each of them staring at their treasure with wide eyes.

Seth walked down the block to get the buggy while Ruthie waited for him on the bench outside the deli. He'd offered to make the trek back and pick her up, hoping she would see what a gentleman he was. As he approached his horse, he noticed Chad engaged in an odd interaction with a young woman who looked familiar to him. Though he couldn't immediately place her, their exchange intrigued him. At first, it seemed as if they were fighting, but the closer he observed them, he could see that Chad had traded a slip of paper for a check. It was then that it clicked in his head.

That's where I know her from; her familye owns The Baker's Dozen Bakery around the corner, and that's the piece of paper Ruthie wrote her recipe on!

CHAPTER SEVEN

"I'm telling you what I saw!" Seth protested. "That's all."

He wasn't trying to come across as being too pushy, but she just wouldn't listen.

"Promise me you won't give him any more of your recipes!" he begged.

"I don't see what the harm is," Ruthie said.

Seth didn't like that Ruthie could be so trusting of Chad, but he was in no position to tell her what to do. She had to make her decisions for herself, but he wished she would listen to him and use caution when dealing with the *Englisher*.

"I hope you don't lose business because of it," Seth cautioned.

"I suppose whatever he does with the recipe is between him and *Gott*," Ruthie said.

Seth blew out a loud and heavy sigh. "I can't argue with that," he relented.

He let his gelding travel along the country road at a slow trot, hoping to gain a little extra time with her. He wanted to explore his new feelings for her, and he didn't want to waste time debating over Chad's morals. In fact, he didn't want to talk about Chad at all.

Lord, help me to let this go for now so I can ask her for a buggy ride.

"I had a nice time at the deli with you; *danki* for letting me treat you."

She giggled and blushed. "It almost seemed like a *date, jah?*"

"*Jah,*" he said with a smile.

Was she baiting him?

It's now or never.

"*Ach,* we could go again sometime—if you want to."

His heart was pounding harder than his gelding's hooves on the pavement.

"I'd like that," she said with downcast eyes.

"I have to go into town on Thursday," he said. "Would you like to come along with me and have lunch again?"

She smiled. "Are you asking me on a *date?*"

She's letting me off the hook! Lord, help me say the right thing.

He let out the breath he'd been holding in.

"Jah, if you want to," he managed.

"If it'll keep you from being jealous of Chad," she said with a giggle. "I'll go on a date with you."

"I'm not jealous," Seth grumbled.

"You are too!"

Seth pushed out his lower lip. "Am not."

Ruthie faced forward and pursed her lips to keep from smiling, her glance darting in his direction a few times before she burst out laughing. "I'm flattered," Ruthie said. "But you have nothing to worry about where Chad is concerned."

Seth's heart skipped a beat. "That's *gut* to know—not that I was worried or anything."

Ruthie wrung her hands while she waited for Seth to show up. She'd been so anxious to go on her date with him she had been beside herself with anticipation. Now that he was about to be here, she was far more nervous than she thought she would be. When she heard buggy wheels coming around the corner, she took in a deep breath and blew it out. Pasting a smile on her nervous face, she tried to convince herself it was only Seth. She'd been to town with him a million times before. This time was different; it was a date. It wasn't a buggy ride, just a date. Would he finally get up the nerve to ask her for a buggy ride? She'd noticed him fidgeting when he'd asked her to have lunch with him, and she'd found it endearing that he was just as nervous as she was.

Seth parked the buggy in the driveway and came up to the porch, a paper bag with handles in his hand.

He approached the porch and handed her the bag. "For your birthday; sorry it's late."

She giggled and took the bag. "You didn't have to get me anything."

"I wanted to," he said shyly.

She sat on one of the wicker chairs on the porch and opened the bag, her breath catching when she pulled out the box containing a water purifying pitcher. "I can't believe you got this! *Danki*."

"All you have to do is fill the pitcher, and it filters through to the bottom, and you have filtered water any time you want," Seth said. "You can put it in the refrigerator to keep it cold."

"That was very thoughtful of you," she said, a lump forming in her throat. It was the most thoughtful gift she'd ever gotten.

"I love it!" she said excitedly. "Now, *Dat* can't get after me for *buying* water!"

Seth chuckled. "You'll have to buy a new filter for it every few months, but we can keep that between us."

She laughed. "*Gut* idea!"

He went in for a hug, and though she'd hugged him before tons of times, it was always as a friend and not as the man she was dating. It felt different, and she liked the butterflies that fluttered in her stomach.

Now that they'd gotten over the awkwardness, she hoped she could just be herself—the way she'd always been with him. He was still the same *comfortable* Seth; only now, she was falling for him.

"Let me put this inside and then we can go," she said. "I'm really hungry."

When they passed by Murdock's Farmer's Market, Chad lifted a hand to wave to them, and Ruthie eagerly waved and smiled, while Seth kept his eyes on the road. It irritated him that Ruthie had waved, and he silently prayed he would get over the jealous feeling trying to creep back into his mind.

"I wonder who that woman was all cozied up to him," Ruthie surprised him in saying.

"That's Robin Baker," Seth answered. "She owns the Baker's Dozen bakery around the corner. I told you I saw him giving her your recipe the other day."

"How do you know her?" Ruthie asked.

"Mei cousin, Albert, asked her out on a date once and she laughed in his face."

Ruthie looked back at the two of them, and Seth had to take in a deep breath to keep from asking her why.

"I guess I understand why you warned me about giving him my recipe," she said, facing forward.

Seth was glad she hadn't noticed the scowl he knew was overtaking his expression. Honestly, he didn't know what was wrong with him; he never felt this way before about any woman. Was this what love does to a man? He couldn't even be sure if what he felt for Ruthie was love, but he knew he couldn't get her off his mind. All he knew was that he wouldn't do anything to mess things up between him and Ruthie. He supposed that alone was a pretty good indication that he loved her.

"I'd like permission to take you for a buggy ride tomorrow evening," he said, clearing his throat. "I know we said lunch today was a date, but having lunch is more for friends, don't you agree? I believe the date—a proper date should involve a buggy ride."

Ruthie smiled. "Funny, but I was just thinking the same thing myself."

Seth clicked at the gelding. "How about we have lunch today as friends and tomorrow night we'll have our first date and I'll take you for a buggy ride."

"I like that idea," she said.

"I'm feeling like a cheeseburger today," Seth said. "Do you want to eat at the diner instead? *Since it's not a date.*"

"*Jah,*" she said with a giggle.

Seth parked the buggy in front of the diner. Then he hopped out and ran around to the side to help Ruthie down from the buggy. Inside the diner, the waitress seated them in a booth near the front window. Seth didn't need a menu to know what he wanted, but he took it anyway. The waitress came back with two glasses of water and silverware, and then pulled out her pad and paper ready to take their order.

"I'll have a cheeseburger with pickles and mustard," Ruthie said. "With fries on the side and a chocolate malt."

Seth smiled. "I'll have the same!"

The waitress took their menus and left them alone at the table.

"Did you decide what you were going to enter for the bake-off contest at the Harvest Festival on Saturday?" Seth asked.

"I think I've decided to enter my harvest whoopie pies—the spicy ones. I was going to enter my pumpkin spice bread, but I think the whoopie pies have a better chance of winning because of the secret ingredient in them!"

Seth raised his eyebrows and smiled. "Secret ingredient, huh?"

Ruthie giggled. "Before you ask, I'm not telling you what it is."

But if Chad asked you for the recipe, I'll bet you'd give it to him!

Seth kept his mouth shut and simply smiled. "I wouldn't think of asking. After all, secret ingredients are supposed to remain secret, aren't they?"

"I am glad you understand," she said. "I wouldn't want such a thing to cause our first argument before we'd had our first date!"

Seth chuckled nervously hoping she wasn't serious. Luckily, the waitress was at their table with their plates of food just in time to interrupt his edgy thoughts about her. He wasn't going to think about why she would say such a thing; all he wanted to do was eat his food and enjoy his afternoon with her. If he could help it, that's what he intended to do.

Seth pulled the buggy into Ruthie's driveway, a feeling of elation after their lunch date. They'd agreed it wasn't their official date, but he knew it was a date, nonetheless. He was so happy; he didn't think anything could change how he felt.

"Hey, isn't that your *mamm* on the porch with *mei dat?*" Ruthie asked.

"*Jah*, they've been seeing a lot of each other lately, aren't they?" Seth asked, a bad feeling twisting in his gut.

"They're becoming *gut* friends," Ruthie said. "I think that is important for them at their age. I know *mei dat* has been awfully lonely, and with Naomi and Jeremiah getting married soon, it will be tough for him—especially when I get married."

Seth got the hint she was dropping, but he didn't like where things were going with his mother and Ruthie's father. He didn't begrudge his mother any happiness, but it was weird now that he was officially dating Ruthie.

He hopped down and helped her out of the buggy, and they walked up to the porch together.

His mother greeted them with a warm smile. He went to her and kissed her cheek.

"I'm so glad you're both here," Ruthie's father said. "We have something we want to tell you."

Seth could feel his knees wobbling. Was he about to announce their engagement? He couldn't marry Ruthie if her father would end up being his step-father; that would be too weird.

He sat, feeling if he didn't, his legs would buckle under him and he'd take a nose-dive onto the porch. Ruthie sat next to him, and he scooted over on the wicker settee, keeping a safe distance from her.

"As you both know," Mr. Yoder began. "*Frau* Troyer and I have been keeping each other's company on a regular basis."

Seth was shaking, and a bead of sweat rolled down the middle of his back.

Please don't say you're getting married.

"I've asked her to marry me this wedding season." The man waited for a response from them, but he didn't get anything except a couple of gasps.

Seth stole a glance at Ruthie, who was as pale as the sheets his *mamm* hangs on the clotheslines. Instinctively, he jumped up and offered his hand to the man who would soon be his step-father.

"Congratulations!" he said, his voice cracking.

Then without looking at Ruthie, he bolted down the stairs.

"I have to go!" he said over his shoulder. "I have chores to finish before dark."

Ruthie ran down the porch steps and was on his heels.

"Wait," she said. "What time are you picking me up tomorrow?"

He turned, unable to look her in the eye. "I'm sorry; I can't take you for a buggy ride. Not tomorrow—not ever."

He hopped in his buggy, slapped the reins and left without another word.

CHAPTER EIGHT

Ruthie stood in the driveway of her father's home, tears filling her eyes as she watched Seth rein his horse down to the main road at breakneck speed.

What just happened?

With one little sentence, her whole world had been pulled out from under her. It wasn't fair. How could their parents do this to them? Unless they counted lunch today, she and Seth hadn't even been able to have their first date, and now it was over between them. She knew why he left, but she wished he'd have given things a chance. Perhaps if they talked, they could figure a way to be together despite the news their parents had dropped in their laps.

Who was she kidding? She knew it was weird. Things would never be the same between them now. She couldn't fall in love with her step brother; it didn't matter that they were both adults. If they didn't still live at home, then it would be different. Lucky for Seth; his mother would be moving in with her *dat,* and she'd be living in the same house with them. But she didn't have to live with them either.

Ruthie ran around the house and went inside through the backdoor despite the fact she could hear her father calling for her. She could pretend she didn't hear him; it wouldn't be the first time she'd ignored him and told him later she simply hadn't heard him calling her.

She ran upstairs to her bedroom and began to pack her things. She had no idea where she was going to live, but it wasn't going to be under the same roof with her father and new step-mother. She cared a great deal for Seth's mother, but that didn't mean she wanted her for a new mother. But wasn't she going to share her with Seth if they would have gotten married?

She sobbed harder.

It didn't matter now; he'd told her he didn't want to date her.

A knock startled her, but she ignored it. She had nothing to say to her father or Seth's mother. They could have each other, but she wasn't going to stick around and be a family with either of them. She'd wanted a family of her own with Seth, and they'd ruined that for her with their announcement.

Another knock followed by the turn of the door knob forced her head around. "Go away, Naomi," Ruthie said through gritted teeth. "I don't want to talk to anyone right know."

"Where're you going?" her sister asked.

She gritted her teeth. "Away from *Dat* and our soon-to-be step-mother!"

Naomi sat on the edge of the bed and began to fold the dresses Ruthie had piled on her bed in a heap. "I think it's wonderful that *Dat* and *Frau* Troyer found each other after all these years."

Ruthie clenched her jaw and bit her bottom lip to keep from crying.

"I know with me and Jeremiah married; it won't be an easy adjustment for you here with another woman in the kitchen," Naomi said. "But that's no reason for you to pack your things and leave. That's *narrish.*"

"Dat is the one who's acting *narrish!"* Ruthie squealed.

"He's been lonely for a long time," Naomi said. "This will be *gut* for him."

Ruthie threw down the dress she was packing and slammed shut the suitcase.

"What about what is *gut* for me?"

Naomi touched her arm. "Move out to the *dawdi haus!* You're all grown now; you don't need a *mudder* to take care of you. I'm sure *Dat* will understand if you want to move out there; what he won't understand any more than I do, is why you want to leave in the first place."

Ruthie burst out crying and slumped onto the end of the bed. "Seth asked me to take a buggy ride with him tomorrow."

Naomi's face lit up. "I had no idea the two of you were serious; I thought he was just helping you with the pumpkin patch."

Ruthie shrugged. "It started out that way. But it doesn't matter anymore; when he heard the news, he lit out of here like he was on fire. But before he left, he said we could never take a buggy ride."

Naomi pulled Ruthie into a hug and let her sob. "I'm so sorry. I had no idea the two of you liked each other that way. It's wonderful, and I'm sure there's a solution to this. It can't be all that bad."

"You didn't see the look on Seth's face," Ruthie sobbed. "He wouldn't even look me in the eye. I don't blame him; I know it will be weird with our parents married."

"It doesn't have to be," Naomi said.

"That's easy for you to say," Ruthie sniffled. "*Dat* isn't marrying Jeremiah's *mamm!*"

Naomi shuddered. *"Ach,* I see your point."

Ruthie's shoulders shook with anguish.

"Give Seth some time; maybe he'll come around after he thinks about it."

Ruthie shook her head. *"Nee,* he's never coming back. Now I'll have to spend Christmas with him as my *step-brother* instead of my husband."

She cried harder, and Naomi tried to shush her.

"You can always run away and get married—and then live at Seth's *haus.*"

"You're not helping!" Ruthie cried. "He doesn't want anything to do with me now, so I need to accept it is over before it began."

"At least stay in the *dawdi haus* instead of leaving," Naomi begged her.

"Nee! I'm going to cousin Beth's; she's been staying in her *dawdi haus* since she turned eighteen. All I know is that I can't stay here another minute."

"Make sure you leave a note for *Dat* giving him some kind of explanation," Naomi suggested.

"Tell him I'm staying over the weekend," Ruthie said. "If I feel better by then,

I'll come home. If not, I'll be staying there until I wear out my welcome."

Ruthie finished packing her things and walked over to her cousin's house without even saying goodbye to her father.

Ruthie sat at the diner with Beth, trying her best not to cry. She glanced at the booth where she and Seth had sat yesterday while she'd listened to one story after another. She'd laughed so hard she could barely eat. Now, she picked at her food and didn't have anything to say.

"I'm sorry I'm such awful company," she said.

Beth waved a hand at her. "I know something that might cheer you up."

Ruthie looked up from the plate of fries that had gotten cold. "What?"

Smiling, Beth pointed behind her. "Don't look, but there is a handsome *Englisher* sitting at the counter, and he's staring at you."

Ruthie shook her head and rolled her eyes. "My face is all puffy from crying; I'm sure he's only staring to make fun of me."

Beth straightened up in her seat and bulged her eyes. "Well, wipe them dry because he's coming this way."

Ruthie sniffled and straightened in her seat when Chad stood beside her.

"Ruthie!" he said with a smile. "I thought that was you; what's wrong? Are you okay?"

She wiped at her face and cleared her throat. "Someone was—burning leaves—and we rode by it—on the way here—and—I'm allergic; I'm sure it will clear up in a few minutes."

He touched her shoulder. "I'm glad to hear you're alright. Will you be at the Harvest Festival tomorrow?"

She cleared her throat again. "*Jah,* I'll be there."

"Great!" he said. "I'm running the kissing booth at two o'clock; come to see me, and I'll save you a kiss!"

Ruthie felt the blood drain from her cheeks when he winked and then waved goodbye to her. She lifted her hand methodically and waved back in a stupor.

Once he was gone, Beth waved a hand in front of her face to get her attention. "What was that? *Who* was that?"

"I'm sorry," Ruthie said, jolting back to reality. "I should have introduced you; that was Chad."

"The one Seth is so jealous of?"

Ruthie nodded sadly. "*Jah,* but it doesn't matter anymore. Seth and I are through."

Beth snapped her fingers in front of Ruthie's face. "Hey, why are you mooning over Seth so much when that guy wants to kiss you?"

"Because his looks are the only thing he has going for him!"

Beth shrugged. "So, what's wrong with that?"

"I want more than that," Ruthie whined. "Seth is handsome and kind, and he loves me—at least I thought he did—until our parents' announcement spooked him like a wild horse."

"So who needs a *mann* with no back bone?" Beth asked.

"It's better than a *mann* with no morals—like Chad," Ruthie complained. "He has a girlfriend—I saw him with her. I think he gave my pumpkin bread recipe to her."

"No wonder Seth is not happy with him," Beth said. "It's too bad because he's really cute. I might have to visit the kissing booth tomorrow at the festival."

That bought a giggle from Ruthie.

"You might try paying him a visit yourself," Beth advised her. "Maybe if Seth sees you kissing another *mann* it will make him jealous enough to come running back to you."

Ruthie shook her head. *"Nee,* Naomi's relationship with Jeremiah nearly ended because of jealousy. And she used Seth to make him jealous, so Seth would see right through that. Besides, I want my first kiss to be with my betrothed; I thought that would be Seth—I want it to be Seth."

Beth sucked in her breath. "You didn't tell me you wanted to kiss Seth! *Ach,* this is serious; we have to find a way to get the two of you back together."

Ruthie pushed the plate of fries away from her. "We were supposed to take our first buggy ride tonight, but I doubt that will happen.

The only way we're going to get back together is if *mei dat* and his *mamm* break up."

Beth put up a finger and opened her mouth to speak, but Ruthie stopped her.

"I'm not going to do anything to hurt *mei dat;* he deserves to be happy. I just wish he would have picked someone else. Of all the widows in the community, why did he have to pick her?"

"Love makes people pick the one who makes their hearts sing," Beth said with a dreamy look in her eyes.

Ruthie sighed. "Don't tell me you're still swooning over Chad."

"If you're not going to, one of us should."

"He's no *gut* for you," Ruthie warned her. "He's nice to look at, but he's an *Englisher,* and I happen to know that he has a girlfriend—though he's tried to hide it from me. She owns the Baker's Dozen Bakery up the street; Seth thinks she's the one he wanted the recipe for."

Beth sucked in her breath. "That's awful!"

Ruthie sipped her milkshake. "Now maybe you understand why he's not so tempting to me anymore."

"You mean he *was* tempting to you at one time?" Beth asked.

"Maybe for about a minute," Ruthie admitted. "But that was before I realized I didn't just want to entertain the idea of being Seth's betrothed—I want to marry that *mann*."

"Well, if you don't want to make him jealous," Beth said. "Then I'm all out of ideas—except to go to him and tell him how you feel."

Ruthie shook her head, discouragement weighing heavily on her heart. "I can't do that—not yet. I think Seth needs some time to process this thing with his *mamm* getting married again. I'll keep him at an arm's length until he's ready to talk to me."

Beth picked up her burger and paused. "Eat your lunch and stop moping; it won't do either of you any *gut*. I guess you know best, but you can stay with me as long as you need to; it gets lonely out there in the *dawdi haus.*"

Ruthie watched her cousin bite into her burger, and it made her stomach growl for the food she'd left on her plate. She was lonely too, and her mind wouldn't stay quiet about Seth long enough to eat anything without crying over him. Her father had always told her that the heart grows fonder in the absence of a loved-one.

He was right. Not only did she miss Seth; she missed her father too.

CHAPTER NINE

Seth pushed himself through his morning chores; he'd skipped out on breakfast to avoid seeing his mother. Last night, he'd eaten in town at the diner after leaving Ruthie in the driveway of her father's house. He was too upset to eat, but he knew he'd be hungry if he didn't, and he wasn't about to sit down to an evening meal with Ruthie and her father after the way he'd run off without giving anyone an explanation.

"If I didn't know better, I'd think you were avoiding me."

His mother's voice startled him.

"You're wrong; I *was* avoiding you, *Mamm,*" Seth confessed. "I'm sorry."

His mother shifted the basket of gourds she'd picked from her garden to her other arm and leaned up against the horse stall where Seth was pitching hay.

"No need to be sorry," she said kindly. "I see things have changed between you and Ruthie; I imagine you're worried about your feelings for her now that I'm marrying her *vadder, jah?*"

He rested his chin on the handle of the pitchfork. "Jah, I think it would be weird between us now, and after the way I ran out on her yesterday, I wouldn't blame her if she never wanted to see me again."

"Maybe if you went and talked to her," his mother suggested.

"*Nee*, I can't date her now—not after the way I reacted…" his voice trailed off.

"Why not?"

"Because she'll be my step sister when you marry her *vadder*."

"Not if you marry her before I marry Abe."

Mamm; you're not helping.

Seth hadn't thought about that, but it wouldn't work either.

"The two of you could live here, and I'll move over to the Yoder *haus* once I marry Abe. That way it won't be weird, and I'll be her *mudder*-in-law before I'm her step-*mudder*."

"You know," Seth said. "That sounds so complicated. Besides, she's probably so mad at me she'll never speak to me again. I really messed this up before it even got started. How can I think of marrying her when we haven't even gone on a date yet?"

"The heart doesn't always want what is logical," his mother said.

That was true enough.

"Does she feel the same way you do?" his mother asked.

Seth didn't have to think about it. "*Jah,* I'm pretty sure she does, but I'm sure I messed it up."

"Then it's worth giving another try, don't you think?" his mother asked before she left the barn.

She'd certainly left him with a lot to think about, but he hadn't missed the stricken look on Ruthie's face when he'd run away like a coward yesterday. It was obvious she felt the same way but he'd probably ruined any chance he had with her. She'd looked at him with loving eyes, and she'd flirted with him a lot in the past week. Would things ever be the same between them?

Tonight was supposed to be their date-night. Did he dare go over to pick Ruthie up as if nothing happened?

"I'm sorry, Ruthie's not here," Naomi said, holding up a hand to Seth. "And before you ask, she told me not to tell you where she was."

He flashed her the *are you serious* look, but it didn't do him any good.

"She needs some time," Naomi warned him. "I think you both need some time to sort this out and see if it's worth pursuing."

Seth ran a hand through his thick blonde hair. "I wouldn't be here if I didn't think she was worth pursuing."

"Sleep on it another night and tell her tomorrow at the Harvest Festival if you still feel the same way."

Seth nodded, feeling lower than he had last night. He knew running away was a mistake as soon as he'd gotten half way down the road; why hadn't he turned around and gone back then? They could have talked things out, and everything would be fine now—wouldn't it? He left the porch, his head hanging from the shame he felt. He hadn't acted like a man; he'd acted like a spoiled child throwing a tantrum because he wasn't getting his way. He'd acted selfishly when he should have been happier for his mother. She'd been lonely for a long time, and she deserved to be happy again. He would not stand in her way—even if it meant he had to give up his own happiness for her sake.

Ruthie woke when the rooster crowed, though she knew she had only closed her eyes a short while ago. She'd tossed and turned and stared at the ceiling most of the night. She needed to get up so she could bake the batch of whoopie pies she intended on taking to the Harvest Festival to enter the bake-off contest. She'd so looked forward to entering for the chance to win the hundred-dollar prize so she and her father would have an easier winter. Now that he was combining households with Seth's mother, she'd bring a lot of canning and foodstuff with her that would get them through the long winter months.

Suddenly feeling as unneeded as a person could feel, she rolled over in the bed, the small, spare room at her cousin's *dawdi haus* making her feel the walls were closing in on her. Was there any point in winning the prize now? She supposed she could give the money to them as a wedding gift, but if she were going to be on her own now, she would also need the money to live on. She couldn't expect her cousin or her *aenti* to support her. She would have to contribute to the household if she intended to stay through the winter. Though she was grateful for a place to stay until she sorted out her life, she missed her own bed and her large room; most of all, she missed the quilt she'd made with her *mamm.*

Dragging herself from the warmth of the quilt that didn't feel like home, Ruthie quickly dressed, ignoring how sleepy she felt; she had too much to do today. Not only that, she wondered how it would be when she ran into Seth at the festival or if he'd even be there. She'd cried half the night over the missed buggy ride with him, and she wished he would have shown up at Beth's to pick her up. She'd been disappointed when he hadn't, but she hadn't expected him to after the way he'd acted two days ago. Had it really been two days since she'd seen him last? Absence had made her heart grow fonder of him, but it had also given her heart ample time to feel the breaking that came along with the absence.

In the small kitchen of the *dawdi haus,* Beth was already up and making a pot of coffee. She would need the entire pot to keep her awake today.

"You look tired," Beth said. "You didn't sleep very well?"

Ruthie shook her head as she un-bagged the ingredients she'd brought over to make her whoopie pies. She'd been grateful Beth had plenty of eggs, butter, and cream, so all she had to pack were the dry ingredients. Sadly, her heart just wasn't in it—not like it was. She'd been so excited to enter and win that money for her and her father, but now it all seemed pointless.

"I'm kind of glad I don't have a boyfriend," Beth said out of the blue.

"Huh?"

Beth put a hand on Ruthie's arm as she handed her a fresh cup of coffee. "You've been staring out the window for the last fifteen minutes!"

Ruthie took the cup of coffee and looked back out the window not realizing the sun had started to come up and she hadn't even noticed.

"Forgive me for being so rude," Ruthie said.

"You're not being rude, but I'm worried about you. You're going to make yourself sick worrying about Seth."

Ruthie sighed as she sat at the kitchen table across from Beth with her coffee. "I think he's the one; how can I get over that?"

"I don't know; I've never been in love before," Beth said. "But if it were me, I'd talk to Seth today and clear things up before you both suffer more hurt than you already are."

Ruthie looked up at her cousin. "Do you think Seth is hurting too?"

"Of course he is; why do you think he reacted the way he did?"

"I guess it seemed to me he reacted that way because he changed his mind—based on our parents' announcement, and it wasn't fair," Ruthie complained. "He should have stayed there and talked about it with me—and maybe with our parents too. I don't know. Everything just happened so fast; I don't know what to think about it anymore—except sad."

"Don't let it get you down; save your worries until after you talk to him."

Ruthie ran her finger around the rim of her empty coffee cup. "What if he won't talk to me?"

Beth shrugged. "Well, I hate to say it, but at least then you'll know."

"What? That it's over?" Ruthie jumped up from her chair and ran back to her small room and threw herself on the bed and began to sob all over again.

If things were over between her and Seth, staying with Beth was not far enough away to avoid running into him. Perhaps she should consider contacting one of her relatives in Ohio.

Ruthie lifted her head from the pillow, her breath hitching. Had she fallen asleep? She glanced at the wind-up clock at the bedside table and grabbed it, panic filling her. She'd fallen asleep; according to the time, she'd slept for two hours.

"I'm going to be late!" she squealed.

She ran into the bathroom and splashed cold water on her face and then ran out to the kitchen where Beth was finishing up the dishes.

Beth turned to look at her. "I was going to wake you as soon as I finished washing this skillet."

"Ach, I can't believe I fell asleep," Ruthie groaned as she poured herself a cup of coffee. "I feel awful, and my head is pounding."

"Sit and drink your *kaffi,* " her cousin said. "I'll dish you up some eggs and bacon; you'll feel better once you get some food in your belly."

"Danki, " she said, sitting at the table. Beth put a plate of food in front of her she'd been keeping warm on the stove and Ruthie bit into the banana walnut muffin still warm from the oven. Her mind reeled with all that she still had to do before getting ready for the festival. She was grateful she'd had the forethought to pull the wagon behind her containing her special pumpkin. She'd stopped in the pumpkin patch and picked it along with a couple of pie pumpkins to make her pumpkin spice whoopie pies. At least she didn't have to run back home to do any of that before she could go today.

"What time do you want to leave for the festival?"

Beth's question pulled Ruthie from her thoughts.

"We'll need to leave by noon," she answered. "The judging begins at two o'clock, and I want to have my pumpkin entry in plenty of time for the judges to get a *gut* look at it."

Beth giggled. "That is an unusual pumpkin; I've never seen another like it. How do you suppose it got all those perfect swirls in it?"

"The best I can figure is that I must have somehow had some seeds from gourds that had mixed with it over the past years of growing in my pumpkin patch. I almost believe it grew up wild from previous years' plantings."

"That amazes me how *Gott* sprouts things up from the soil," Beth said. "Do you remember that huge cucumber Seth found in his garden last summer that was as big as a large zucchini? That thing must have weighed..." her voice trailed off. "I'm sorry; I didn't mean to bring up Seth."

Ruthie pushed her plate back, her stomach suddenly in knots. It was going to be a long day, and she wasn't looking forward to running into Seth at the festival.

CHAPTER TEN

Ruthie jumped from Beth's buggy and ran around the back to get her pumpkin.

"Promise me you'll get there on time!" she said to Beth. "I have to take my pumpkin; if I drop it along the way, it's on me, but if you dropped it—well, I'd have someone to be upset with other than myself."

"Don't worry," Beth assured her. "I'll get your whoopie pies entered, and I'll guard them with my life!"

Ruthie paused. "I'm being dramatic, aren't I?"

Beth held up two fingers in a pinch. "Just a little bit, but I understand; you could win big prize money with both of these entries, and that would give you enough money to get a fresh start in life."

Ruthie cradled her pumpkin in her arms and paused again briefly. She hadn't thought about using the money to get away from here, but it gave her hope that she wouldn't have to stick around and watch Seth marry someone else instead of her.

"Wish me luck!" she said.

Beth shooed her with her hand. "You don't need it, but I wish it for you just in case!"

"*Danki*," Ruthie said as she walked over toward the pumpkin judging area before they closed the entries.

"Last call for pumpkin entries," she heard the announcer call.

"Wait!" Ruthie called out, walking as fast as she could without risking dropping her pumpkin.

She slowed down to a safe pace when the man saw her approaching with her large pumpkin in her arms.

By the time she reached the stand, she was sweating and out of breath. But she'd made it just in time.

"That's a unique pumpkin you have there," the man said.

Ruthie smile proudly. "*Danki*."

"You got it here just in time," he said pointing to the judges, who had already begun to examine the first pumpkin at the end of the long table. She had to walk away; she couldn't stand around and watch them judge her pumpkin. She left her name with her entry and began to look for the bake-off canopy. It wasn't that she didn't trust Beth to get it there on time; she needed to see for herself in order to have peace of mind.

Once she located the tent where the bake-off was being held, Beth was nowhere around. Ruthie had a good idea where she could find her cousin, and she was certain the girl's trail of popcorn would lead straight to the kissing booth and Chad Murdock. If only her problems could be that easily remedied. She located her whoopie pies among the many entries and double-checked her name card. Curious, she decided to size up the competition. Some items looked as if they might come in second place, but none looked like they would give her entry a run for the money—until the last entry at the end of the table.

She drew in a breath and held it there while she read the name on the card. It was

Robin Baker; wasn't the name of the woman Seth had told her about that owned the bakery around the corner from the park? If she wasn't mistaken, that pumpkin bread was her recipe; she could smell the anise extract which was her *secret* ingredient. Even the icing was the same drizzled pattern, and the powdered sugar was lightly sprinkled on top just the way Ruthie did. It was as if she'd made a replica of the pumpkin bread she'd taken to the Murdock's Farmer's Market. Unless this one *was hers;* she could have frozen it until today and thawed it especially for the bake-off. Surely, she wasn't that underhanded, was she?

She paused in front of the regulator of the contest, wondering if she should say something to him. What would she say? That she *thinks* that pumpkin bread is hers? No, she'd make a spectacle of herself and probably get her whoopie pies disqualified for poor sportsmanship. She drew in another breath and held it in until her anger subsided. It was best to keep quiet. If the girl were to win instead of

143

Ruthie, then, and only then, would she make a fuss about it. She chuckled inwardly that she likely had two entries in the bake-off and she wondered if that was against the rules. It didn't matter; if the pumpkin bread won first prize, it would go to Robin and not her.

Life seems to be dealing me some unfair turns, Lord; is there a lesson to be learned in all of this?

She walked away, leaving the outcome in God's hands; it was just as much out of her control as the situation with Seth, both of which would drive her crazy if she didn't let them go and let God handle them. She didn't have the power to solve her problems; all she could do was wait on God for the answer.

Up ahead, she spotted her father with Seth's mother, but still no sign of Seth. Her heart raced as they waved and walked toward her. She hadn't seen her father in the two days since she'd packed her things and left without saying goodbye to him. She'd acted just like

Seth; he didn't appear to be upset with her, but what if he waited to reprimand her until *Frau* Troyer was not with him. Ruthie pasted on a smile and welcomed them both with a brief hug.

"Did Seth find you yet?" *Frau* Troyer asked.

Ruthie shook her head; Seth was looking for her?

"I know he wanted to talk to you," she said. "I think the two of you will feel a lot better about things once you work out your differences."

Our differences? More like the wrench you and mei vadder threw in our lives.

"In the meantime," her father said. "I'd like a moment with you alone."

Here it comes; the big lecture.

Frau Troyer walked over to the hay-stacking contest in progress in a roped off area not far from where they were standing, leaving

145

her alone with her father. Thankfully, the contest was drawing a large, noisy crowd, and she prayed it would be loud enough that no one would hear her getting an earful from her father about the way she left the other day.

"*Dat*, I'm sorry for leaving the way I did, but…" she began, hoping if she apologized, he would go easier on her.

"My only concern right now is wondering if you're alright," he interrupted her.

What? Was her father concerned only for her?

"What do you mean, *Dat*?" she asked.

"I know our announcement made you and Seth uncomfortable, and it was probably a big shock, but we don't want to hurt either of you. We can wait to get married until the end of the season to give you and Seth a chance to reconcile," her father said.

Now I feel even worse!

Ruthie shook her head. "*Nee*, you and the Widow Troyer deserve to be happy, and I think you should be the first couple to be married this season. I want you to be happy, Dat, and I'll stay out of your newlywed hair by staying with Beth. I won't be far away, I promise."

Her father smiled, tears filling his eyes. "Your *mudder* would have been proud to see what a *gut* young woman you've turned out to be." He handed her an envelope. "This is for you—from your *mudder;* I think it's time for this one."

Ruthie grabbed the letter excitedly; it was her second letter—the first, she'd gotten on her birthday just weeks ago. "May I read it now?"

Abe pulled his daughter into a hug. "Read it before you go and talk with Seth."

"But I wasn't planning on talking…"

"Talk to him," her father interrupted. "He's hurting too, and I think the two of you need to work this out—one way or the other."

"You're right, *Dat,*" she said. "I'll read this—and then I'll go talk to him."

Her father left her, and she sat against a large oak tree in the grass among the colorful leaves that had fallen from its branches. She opened the letter and began to read.

Tears filled her eyes at the lovely words her mother had written to her, but her focus locked onto one phrase.

When it comes to love, the heart wants what the heart wants; always follow your heart, and you will never go wrong.

Her heart was telling her to follow Seth, and it was stronger than she'd ever imagined it could be. Her heart wanted to marry him and have a family with him.

Lord, let Seth's heart match my heart so we can be married—if it is your will.

CHAPTER ELEVEN

Seth looked for Ruthie at the bake-off tent; her entry was there, but she wasn't. Wondering if he should hang around to see if she would show up to see how the judging was coming along, he noticed a loaf of pumpkin bread at the opposite end of the table. The card in front of the bread showed the name *Robin Baker*. Panic filled him as he remembered seeing Chad giving the bakery owner Ruthie's recipe. If she'd made it exactly to Ruthie's recipe, it was highly likely she would win the bake-off. Then he realized that it had been put forward with what looked like some sort of cake. The judges were more than halfway through the tasting process, and they'd placed what he was certain was Ruthie's pumpkin bread in the lead.

How would Ruthie take it if Robin won the bake-off with her recipe? It would break her heart. Should he tell the judges about his suspicions? No; he had no proof the recipe belonged to Ruthie. He also didn't have the heart to tell Ruthie about it. There wouldn't be any cause to alert Ruthie unless her whoopie pies lost to her pumpkin bread recipe. He supposed if Robin did the actual baking, it would likely be considered as her entry, and it probably wouldn't matter to the judges whose recipe it was. It mattered to him, and he was determined to discover the truth. First, he would confront Chad, and if necessary, he'd go to Robin directly.

One way or another, the two of them would make it up to Ruthie, and he would make sure of it. He'd let her down in the worst way, and though his defending her to Robin and Chad wouldn't come close to making up for what he'd done, he was prepared to do whatever it took to win her back.

As he walked around the droves of people, Seth spotted Ruthie near the pumpkin-judging area, her smile wide enough to break his heart. He loved her more than he thought he did; there was no way he could live without her. But would she still have him after the way he'd acted? He was prepared to face the consequences of his actions, and if her answer was no, he'd have to live with that. What he couldn't live with was never telling her how he feels and never giving her the chance to accept his apology. It wouldn't be easy, but he had to believe that *Gott* brought them together for a reason, and for him, that reason was love.

He continued to walk toward her, practicing in his head what he would say to her when he reached her. Would it be enough?

Chad was suddenly at her side, and Seth stopped in his tracks. He stood back and watched to see how she would handle herself with him. That, and if she needed help, he'd be close-by. At least that's what he was trying to convince himself of instead of the obvious; he was spying on Ruthie and Chad, and it made him feel awful.

He would hold back for a little while and let the two of them talk; she seemed to enjoy talking to him for some reason, but Seth didn't care for him.

"Seth," he heard his sister, Katie's voice behind him. "*Mamm* was looking for you."

He turned his attention from Chad and Ruthie long enough to look at his sister and answer. "I've already talked to her a couple of times today; when did she say she wanted to talk to me?"

"About five minutes ago."

"I'll look for her in a minute," he said, looking back toward the pumpkin table.

Ruthie and Chad were gone.

Ruthie followed Chad over to the games area; she and Seth usually entered the three-legged race, but she doubted they would enter this year. She didn't want to even watch for fear it would only upset her, but she hadn't seen Seth yet, and she was losing confidence that she'd see him today. His mother had mentioned he wanted to talk to her, but he didn't seem like he was trying very hard to find her.

"Are you sure you don't want to enter the race?" Chad asked. "It looks like fun."

Ruthie shrugged. "Maybe later; I'm anxious to see how the bake-off is going and if they've finished judging my pumpkin yet."

"I'm sure you'll win the bake-off," Chad said. "And I'm not just saying that because I'm such a fan of your baking. And I've seen that pumpkin; if I hadn't seen for myself it was real, I'd think you were entering a decoration that you painted yourself. I've never seen a pumpkin that looked quite like it."

"*Danki,*" Ruthie said. "For trying to cheer me up."

"Cheer you up?" Chad asked. "I noticed you're not with your *friend*—Seth, is it? Did something happen between you two?"

Ruthie bit her bottom lip.

"Did he break up with you?"

"*Nee,* it's not like that," she said.

Chad put a finger under her chin and looked her in the eye. "Are you okay? You seem sad."

Why was he prying? Were all *Englishers* like that?

"I'm fine," she fibbed pulling gently away from him.

"If you ever need anyone to talk to, I'm a good listener—so I'm told."

"*Danki.*"

She felt a rush of arms behind her. "They judged the pumpkins!" Beth squealed. "Hurry; you have to come and see."

"Did I win?" Ruthie asked; she wasn't sure she wanted to know the answer.

"I don't know," Beth said, pulling her to go with her. "I heard the announcer and came running to find you."

Chad went along with them to the tent where she'd left her pumpkin in the hands of the judges, though she wasn't sure if she wanted him tagging along. She let it go because she was too excited to see how her pumpkin had fared.

As she approached, Seth was standing near her pumpkin; her heart swelled when she caught his smile. From the corner of her eye, she noticed Beth grabbing Chad's arm and looping her arm in his, holding him back. Ruthie continued toward Seth, her heart pounding, her steps seemingly taking her to him in slow motion. The rest of the world magically slipped away, the noise of the people surrounding them suddenly drowned out and became muffled. All she could see was Seth, his smile, and his waiting arms.

She ran to him and flung herself into his arms not caring who was watching; she loved him, and she didn't want to be apart from him again. He flung her around, and she giggled happily.

"I missed you!" Seth whispered in her ear.

"I missed you too!" she said with a giggle.

He put her down, and he pulled her by the hand to look at her pumpkin that boasted a large blue ribbon.

"I got first place!" she squealed.

Seth kissed her gently on the cheek, and their gaze froze on each other momentarily until Beth and Chad were suddenly on the backs of their necks.

"You did it," Beth squealed. "You won!"

Ruthie and Seth each moved, putting a sizeable gap between them.

"Congratulations!" Chad said.

Ruthie forced a smile for him. *"Danki."*

They waited around for the man running the booth to give her the prize money.

Chad's phone rang, and he excused himself to take the call. The last thing he wanted was for Ruthie to overhear the conversation between him and Robin that he knew would not be a pleasant call. She'd been texting him the past ten minutes, demanding he meet her at the bake-off tent. He knew by her mad emoji faces in the messages that she likely had not won the bake-off.

"What is so important that you couldn't wait a minute?" he asked Robin with a low growl.

"Because I've been watching you getting all cozy with that Amish girl for the last hour and I'm over it," Robin screamed at him from the other end.

Chad scoffed at her. "Yeah, I'm real cozy with her while her boyfriend is standing right there."

He didn't admit to the girl that he was hoping Ruthie's breakup with Seth was a permanent one, but they seemed to make up quickly over her prize-winning pumpkin. If that was all it took for them to mend fences, Chad knew he didn't stand a chance with her. He didn't know why he liked her so much, but he supposed it was her gentle honesty. She was better off with Seth; he would love her the way a man should, whereas Chad was only interested in a date to satisfy his curiosity about her. Seth was the one who loved her, and she deserved to have someone love her; she was an awesome person.

"Chad!" Robin was screaming into the phone.

"What?" he asked, taking his eyes off Seth and Ruthie, who were only a few yards away from him.

"Have you even heard a word I said to you?"

"About what?" he asked.

"I want you to get that recipe from the Amish girl," Robin barked.

"What recipe?"

She growled. "I knew you weren't listening!" she squealed. "She won the bake-off with her stupid whoopie pies!"

Chad laughed. "Good! I'm glad to hear that she won; it serves you right for trying to cheat with her recipe."

A high-pitched scream caused Chad to pull the phone away from his ear.

"I'm going to pretend you didn't just say that to me," she screeched. "Get me that prize-winning recipe for those whoopie pies from the Amish Girl for me. I need those for my bakery."

"I'll do no such thing!" Chad said.

"Then I'll tell her you gave me the first recipe!" Robin said.

"Now you're going to strong-arm me into doing your dirty work?" Chad asked. "Why don't you get it from her yourself?"

"Because you're the one who has a crush on her!"

Chad felt his face heat. "I don't have a crush on her; I wanted to get to know her better, but she's got a boyfriend, and I won't get in the middle of that. She loves him—not me, and she's not going to give me another recipe."

"Tell her it's for your mommy again like you did the first time!"

"My mother isn't here," Chad said. "and I probably won't see Ruthie again; she won't be bringing us anymore pumpkins."

"So order some from her," Robin demanded. "Thursday is Halloween; tell her you need them, and when she shows up with the pumpkins, you tell her your mother asked for the recipe when you told her she won first prize at the bake-off."

"She wasn't planning on bringing me anymore pumpkins," Chad said. "What if she doesn't have any left?"

"Then you'll have to think of something else," Robin barked. "I don't care how you get it, but you better get me that prize-winning recipe or I'll tell her you sold me her bread recipe. How do you think she'll feel about you when she finds out you sold her recipe?"

"Her boyfriend will come with her to bring the pumpkins," Chad said. "I won't be able to ask her about the recipe if he's standing right there; I think he already suspects me."

"That's your problem!" Robin said just before she hung up on him.

Chad's shoulders sagged as he watched Ruthie and her cousin giggling and talking. He was envious of the closeness Seth had with her—not because he was in love with her, but because she was an angel compared to Robin.

CHAPTER TWELVE

NAOMI greeted Ruthie at the bake-off tent. "Did you see if you won yet?" her sister asked.

Ruthie shook her head and smiled, her hand tucked securely in Seth's. It didn't matter to her if she won, though she suspected the prize money would come in handy their first winter together if he should ask her to marry him this wedding season. She prayed he would, but first things first; she was eager to see if she won the bake-off.

They all walked into the tented area where all the baked-goods decorated the tables. It didn't take Ruthie long to spot the blue ribbon in front of the nearly empty plate with her name card in front. Her breath hitched, and Seth squeezed her hand.

"I can't believe both my entries won first prize!" she said proudly.

"I had faith in you," Naomi said. "Now, maybe you'll come home where you belong. The supper table isn't the same without your constant chatter."

"You'll be moving away soon," Ruthie complained. "And *Dat* will be married; nothing is going to be the same ever again."

Naomi hugged Ruthie. "I'll practically be in the back yard of *Dat's haus* since *Mamm* sold that piece of land to Jeremiah. I won't be far, and *Dat* getting married is a *gut* change."

"I know," Ruthie said. "But it makes me happy and sad at the same time; the whole thing is so confusing."

"No need to be confused, little *schweschder. Ach,* I'll still be in your hair—probably so much you'll get sick of me."

"I could never get sick of seeing you, Naomi. But I guess this is all part of being a grownup. No wonder *Mamm* said we should be careful what we wished for because when we get it, it might not be what we expected—or wanted."

Naomi pulled her into another hug. "You'll want the changes that are coming your way, Ruthie." She smiled, darting her gaze between her sister and Seth. "I have a feeling we'll be planning your wedding soon, too."

"I think Seth is going to ask if he can give me a ride home from the baptismal classes on Sunday night," Ruthie whispered to her sister.

Naomi smiled. "I'm so pleased to hear that you'll be joining me and Jeremiah at the baptismal classes. Are you sure you're ready to join the church?"

Ruthie nodded. "*Jah,* I'm as sure of that as I am that I want Seth to ask me to marry him."

They both giggled and then joined the others, who had crowded around her blue ribbon. In the background, Ruthie caught sight of the mean glare from Robin Baker, and it made her heart drum against her ribs in an uneven rhythm.

She felt Seth's hand in hers once again, and he gave it a light squeeze as if to let her know he was there for her.

"Chad, *Darling*!" Robin gushed. "I was looking all over for you."

Chad turned to Ruthie and Seth. "I'd like you to meet Robin…"

"Let's go!" Robin said, jerking his arm.

Chad hesitated, barely able to look them in the eye. "I've got to go," he said timidly. "Congratulations, Ruthie on your win."

"Danki."

Robin nudged him, and he cleared his throat. "Ruthie, um, would it be possible for you to bring me another load of pumpkins on Monday?"

Her gazed darted between Chad and Robin, and she thought it was odd how nervous he seemed.

"*Jah,* I'll bring some more pumpkins," she said. "How many do you need?"

"Is twenty-five too many?" he asked, his voice cracking.

Robin smirked, and she felt the girl was up to something, but she ignored her. "*Nee,* I have more than that in my pumpkin patch if you want them."

Chad shook his head. "I don't think I have room for more than twenty-five; they'll be a real life saver."

Robin squeezed his arm and growled at him. "C'mon," she said through gritted teeth. "Smells like a pig farm around here and I want to go home."

Chad put up an apologetic hand to wave to them and mumbled a quiet goodbye; Ruthie didn't miss the forlorn look in his eyes. She didn't understand why he would even go with her if he loathed her so much, but she supposed he had to have his reasons.

Ruthie waved back without a word, thinking she almost felt sorry for him.

"Why were you so rude to them?" Chad said to Robin once they were out of earshot of Ruthie and Seth. "Do you think she's going to give me that recipe now after the way you insulted them?"

"You better make sure she does," Robin warned him, or I'll tell her everything and how it was *your* idea for me to use her recipe to enter that bake-off."

Chad pulled his arm away from hers. "I'll get this recipe for you, and after that, I don't ever want to see you again."

Robin threw her head back and laughed. "I own you now, so you'll be playing by *my rules*. I'm going to be a part of your life until I get tired of you or I have no more use for you, so you better get used to seeing me around."

Chad threw his hands up in defeat, but his mind was reeling with a way out of this. He had until Monday to figure a way out of the mess he'd gotten himself into with Robin before he had to hurt Ruthie again. He didn't want to steal her recipes for Robin. Admittedly, he'd done the wrong thing by getting it in the first place. He'd played along with Robin's games, but afterward, he'd felt bad for what he did to Ruthie. She'd been so nice to him; Robin was nice at first too, and he might have loved her at one time, but it was over between them the minute he'd gone along with Robin's plan to stab Ruthie in the back.

"I meant what I said," Chad said, standing his ground.

Robin smirked. "We'll just see about that."

Ruthie had her arms full carrying her prize-winning pumpkin and both her blue ribbons, but she couldn't be prouder. "It's been a long day, but it was fun."

"Let me carry the pumpkin for you," Seth offered. "I promise I won't drop it."

"*Ach,* it doesn't matter if you drop it now," she said with a giggle. "I'm going to cut it open and get the seeds so I can grow them on purpose next season!"

Seth chuckled. "I imagine you'll get another prize winner out of the patch next year then."

"I have to stop by Beth's house and get my things," she said.

"I thought that was where I was taking you," Seth said.

"*Nee,* I need to go home where I belong," Ruthie said sadly. "I think I hurt *mei vadder* when I left, and I need to make that up to him and show him that I support his decision to marry your *mudder.*"

"*Ach,* I talked with the two of them earlier today when I first arrived at the festival. It was strange to me at first, and I wondered how it would affect you and me, but I'll get *mei vadder's haus* when *mei mudder* moved in with your *vadder* after they are married, so I will have a place to bring my bride and raise a *familye.*"

Ruthie felt her cheeks heat up thinking about she and Seth raising a family at his farm. It was a wonderful dream, and he hadn't exactly asked her yet, but she had a feeling he was going to very soon.

When they reached her driveway, they'd managed to talk the entire ride home about her pumpkin: that, and Robin's expression when she saw Ruthie's blue ribbon from the bake-off. There was no way to prove she'd used Ruthie's pumpkin bread recipe to go up against her for the prize money, but Ruthie suspected it was more about that ribbon where Robin was concerned. She supposed having a blue-ribbon item in her bakery would help business for her but cheating and stealing was no way to win anything in life. Ruthie thanked God that the girl's evil ways did not earn her a reward, for she needed that money far more than the spoiled bakery owner who seemed to lack morals.

Seth parked the buggy and jumped down to help Ruthie out and to get her pumpkin from the back.

"Are you going to the baptismal classes that start tomorrow night after church services?" Seth asked.

"*Jah,* I plan to take the baptism," she said, hoping he knew what that meant for the two of them.

"I'm glad to hear that," he said. "May I take you home after class tomorrow night?"

They'd missed their date, but Ruthie was aware that his offer to bring her home from the baptismal classes was more than a date; it was an offer to court her.

She smiled. *"Jah,* I'd like that."

CHAPTER THIRTEEN

NAOMI helped Ruthie take her things upstairs to her room. "Where's *Dat?*"

"He and *Frau* Troyer left the festival early," Naomi answered. "I believe he is taking supper at her *haus* this evening."

"Seth and I had a hotdog at the festival—and a long talk over it."

Naomi began to put her things away. "Did you work everything out?"

Ruthie sat on her bed and ran her hand over the quilt she and her mother had made together. "*Jah,* he asked me if he could take me home after the baptismal classes tomorrow night."

Naomi stopped hanging up her sister's dresses and went over to the bed and sat down beside her, a grin wider than Ruthie had ever seen on her. "Everyone knows that a ride home from the classes is as *gut* as a proposal of marriage."

"I know!" Ruthie admitted. "I guess it means we could be married this wedding season too!"

Naomi laughed. "Who would have thought that you and I would be married the same season as our *vadder?*"

"*Ach,* that is pretty funny when you say it like that," Ruthie said. "But I'm truly happy for him and Seth's *mamm.*"

"*Jah,* me too," Naomi said. "And I'm really happy to hear that it won't be a problem for you and Seth."

"*Nee,* I was worried after Seth's reaction at first, but when we saw each other today, we realized how much we missed each other—even if we could only be friends."

"It sounds to me that you will be getting a proposal soon," Naomi said excitedly.

They both giggled until they heard a buggy pull up into the driveway.

"*Dat's* home!" Ruthie said. "I have to talk to him; do you mind putting away the rest of my things? I have some more apologizing to do."

Naomi nodded knowingly, and Ruthie pulled in a deep breath before going downstairs to meet her father.

Ruthie patted the envelopes containing her prize money in the pocket of her apron, hoping the peace offering would be enough to smooth over what she'd done. She reasoned with herself that she was an adult and could leave home if she wanted to, but the way she'd handled herself was wrong, and for that, she owed her father an apology. If he wanted to, he could refuse her to come home, but her father had never been a harsh man—even though he pretended to be strict with her and Naomi a lot of their growing years. They both knew that beneath his gruff exterior was the heart of a good father who loved his daughters and only wanted the best for them. He'd proved it repeatedly in the way he'd loved their mother all the way up to the end of her life.

Ruthie thought of her mother now more than ever and wished she could be here to share her special moments that were about to happen in her life, but she knew now that God was blessing her with a new mother to share all those moments. Not only that, but her father was happy again, and she wouldn't do anything to take that away from him. He deserved to be happy, and she would never do anything to stand in the way of that happiness because he would do the same for her.

She stood in the kitchen and waited for her father to come in from the barn after putting away the horse. Needing something to do with her idle hands instead of pacing and wringing them, she put on a pot of coffee, hoping it would be a welcome gift after being out in the cold night. The temperature had dropped drastically since she'd been back home, and she suspected it was the turn of the season that would bring winter upon them before long.

She stared out the window at the multi-colored leaves that tossed around the yard in the wind. The trees were nearly bare already, and the night sky looked as if it could bring down a batch of snow. Would her pumpkins survive if it were to snow? If they didn't, Chad wouldn't get the last of the pumpkins from her patch, and for some reason, she was okay with that. It would bring in another twenty-five dollars for her, but she wondered if it was worth the hassle of forcing Seth to keep his company again. Seth didn't hate Chad, but he didn't trust him either, especially since they'd all suspected Robin had used her pumpkin recipe to enter the bake-off. She could have only gotten the recipe from one person, and that was Chad.

Ruthie shrugged off the worry knowing God would take care of things in his own way, and if that meant snow destroyed the remains of her pumpkin patch, she would accept that it was for her own good.

The coffee pot began to percolate; it would only be a few minutes before she would have hot coffee ready for her father when he exited the barn. She knew the coffee would finish brewing before she'd see him come from the barn; he was always very thorough with his horse when bedding him down for the night—especially on a cold night like tonight was turning out to be. She shivered a little as she watched the wind toss around the leaves that littered their yard. Pulling her shawl around her with one hand, she pulled down two coffee cups from the cabinet with the other. Then she went to the refrigerator for the homemade pumpkin spice creamer she'd mixed up. It was almost gone; she'd have to make another batch with the pie pumpkins she'd put up in the cellar. She hadn't bothered to pick the decorative pumpkins because they grew so sparsely in the patch. She'd grown mostly pie pumpkins to make her bread and whoopie pies, and the pumpkin cookies her father loved so much.

Ruthie pulled in a deep breath when she saw her father exit the barn and blew it out as she lifted the coffee pot to pour them a cup. She stirred in the creamer and set them on the table when her father walked in through the mudroom.

His face lit up when he saw the coffee waiting for him. "Let me get out of these boots, and I'll join you."

Ruthie sat down, happy that her father seemed to be in a good mood. It was to her advantage if she could keep him that way. If she upset him, he might not be as willing to let her return home as she prayed he would.

"It looks like we might get some snow overnight," she commented casually.

He sat across from her and wrapped his hands around the cup of hot coffee, bringing it to his shivering lips with both hands. "*Jah,* did you come back for your pumpkins?"

She slowly lifted the envelopes from her apron pocket and slid them across the table.

He looked at her with a long pause. "What is this?"

"I won first prize for *mei* pumpkin and *mei* whoopie pies in the bake-off!"

"Congratulations!" Her father opened the envelopes and raised an eyebrow at the contents. "That is a lot of money; you need to keep it in a safe place."

He pushed it back toward her, but she stopped him by putting her hand over his. "I want you to have it—for your marriage to *Frau* Troyer."

A smile crossed his lips, and he nodded. "I appreciate the gesture, but you don't need to butter me up; I didn't let your *schweschder* turn your room into a sewing room, so you can have it back if you want it."

She jumped up and flung her arms around her father's neck. "*Danki, Dat;* I'm so sorry for the way I ran out of here a couple of days ago."

He waved a hand at her. "It's already forgotten."

CHAPTER FOURTEEN

Seth tuned out the Bishop while he began class; he was too busy thinking about the buggy ride home with Ruthie and what he would say to her.

"We will begin each class with reading through the eighteen articles from the *Dordrecht* Confession of Faith," the Bishop said. "We will have time to review a few articles each class over the next few weeks."

Seth glanced to the right of him where Ruthie sat, hanging on every word the Bishop was saying. He had no idea she was so serious about her baptism. He respected that, knowing she would make him a good wife when the time came. Truthfully, for him, he was still on the fence about his baptism, but he would never tell her that. It didn't make any difference to him; he would go through the motions for her—if it meant he could marry her. Being a few years older than Ruthie, Seth had let several wedding seasons pass him by without considering the baptism for a single woman—until Ruthie melted his heart. For her, he would take the baptism and become a member of the church. His commitment to God had nothing to do with the church or the *Ordnung,* though he would never admit that to her or anyone else. It didn't matter to him where he worshiped from; he could worship on a mound of dirt, and it would mean the same to him. God was the center for him, and Ruthie was second in his heart—as it should be. For some, the baptism meant simply joining the church—to him, it was his commitment to his faith in God and Amish or not, reciting the rules of the *Ordnung* would not change his view on God or his faith the way some of the youth protest.

Right now, he was content to admire Ruthie's devotion that would allow the two of them to marry in the church, and he was happy it was just as important to her as it was to him.

At the conclusion of their first class, Seth didn't waste any time rushing to Ruthie's side. He was so eager to take her for their long-awaited buggy ride he thought he might burst.

They exited the building, and a burst of cold air brought swirls of light snowflakes in through the open doorway. Seth was glad he'd had the sense to pack a couple of lap quilts in his buggy; he'd anticipated the cold weather but had no idea they'd be getting flurries too. The light wisps of snow would only add to the romantic night he had planned for him and Ruthie.

She lifted her eyes to the swirling snow fluttering down from the heavens. "I love this time of the year; the first snow is always so magical."

"I thought for sure and for certain we would be snowed in this morning when we got up, but the sun was shining, and not a sign of the white stuff," Seth said. "I'm glad it waited until tonight; it's a bit romantic, don't you think?"

He tucked his arm around her, and she giggled as they made their way to his buggy. Seth helped her up onto the seat of the open buggy and tucked two lap quilts around her.

"I brought mittens," she said, pulling them from the pocket of her coat.

Seth chuckled as he climbed up beside her in the buggy. "Smart girl; I brought an extra pair *mei mudder* gave to me—just in case, but I would have kept them warm by holding them if need be."

Ruthie giggled again and stuffed her mittens back in her pockets. "I like your idea better," she said, slipping her hands into his free hand.

He slapped the reins and set his horse on the path toward Goose Pond, where they would sit under the stars and talk about their future while they watched the snowflakes dancing around them.

"I wanted to let you know that I patched things up with *mei dat,*" she said.

"That's *gut;* I'm happy to hear that," Seth said. "Will you be going back to Beth's *haus* once our parents are married?"

"Jah, and *mei dat* understands that. I think it will make things easier."

Seth steered the buggy to a quiet spot at the edge of the public access to the pond. Others had picked the spot to park their buggies under the stars tonight, and he wanted as much privacy with Ruthie as he could get. The crickets were quiet, and so were the frogs; most of the birds had flown south for the winter, and the ones that remained were silent. The only thing they could hear was the whistling of the wind and the fluttering of light snowflakes that melted on their warm cheeks.

Ruthie leaned into Seth's sturdy frame as he tucked an arm behind her. She shivered; some from nerves, and the rest from the chill in the air. She was enjoying his closeness; in his arms was the only place she wanted to be right now—and for the rest of her life. Did she dare tell him that? He'd taken so long to ask her for a buggy ride. She feared she'd have another birthday before he asked her to marry him. She didn't want to be the sort of woman who would push her man; she would be quiet and wait for him. She nuzzled his neck a little, the hair on the back of her neck standing on end. She suspected it wasn't only from the cold but from the excitement of having her mouth so close to his skin. She could easily kiss him right now; would it prompt him to kiss her on the mouth?

She didn't want to come across as forward, but she was ready to explore a deeper closeness with him—one that would eventually lead to the closeness they would experience once they were married. It had to start with a first kiss, and she was more than ready; would he pick up on her signal?

She nuzzled a little closer and pressed her face so close to his neck she could smell the fresh scent of peppermint soap on his skin. He pulled her close, seemingly taking the hint, and she pressed her lips softly to his neck. He tucked his face in her neck and began to kiss her neck and along her jawline and over to her ear, causing her to lean her head back and let his lips take over. She closed her eyes against the tickle she felt when his lips swept across her cheek, her breath shallow and rapid.

Finally, his lips swept across hers with an exhilaration she never expected. She lost all thoughts except for the feel of his warm lips taking the chill from her. The love in her heart for Seth ignited a fire in her heart that resonated through her veins like warm bath water. It was soothing and comforting in a way that made her feel her heart had found a home in him.

"I want to marry you, Ruthie," Seth said quietly and almost out of breath.

Ruthie's breath caught in her throat. Though she'd expected it, hoped for it, and especially prayed for it, his statement still sent a wave of shock through her.

"I want to marry you too, Seth," she managed with a half-whisper.

Seth smiled and resumed kissing her, and she thought she could kiss him all night.

Ruthie tip-toed through the house and went up to Naomi's room; she didn't expect her to be asleep yet since she'd ridden home with

Jeremiah and had likely gotten home almost as late as she had. She knocked lightly, though she was so anxious to talk to her sister, she didn't wait for her to answer. Naomi was turning down the covers and looked up when Ruthie entered.

She hurried to her sister's bed and threw herself onto the mattress on her back and stared at the ceiling. "He asked me!" she said dreamily.

Naomi fluffed her pillow. "To marry him?"

Ruthie bolted upright and smiled, bouncing from the mattress. *"Jah;* he asked me to marry him!"

Naomi pulled Ruthie into a hug, and they both squealed and then shushed each other. It was too late; they heard the footfalls of their father coming down the hall.

"What is all the noise in here so late at night," he asked in a gruff voice.

He covered his mouth, but Ruthie could see the smile he tried to hide.

"Seth asked me to marry him, *Dat!*" Ruthie squealed.

He moved his hand away from his face revealing a full smile. "I had a feeling you would be getting a proposal tonight," he said. "That is why I stayed up; I heard the buggy drive up to the *haus.* So he asked you, then; I'm happy for you."

She ran to her father who stood in the doorway and flung her arms around him. He pulled her into a hug and then let out a chuckle. "This means you will want this!" He handed her a letter with her mother's handwriting on it.

She let out a squeal and took the letter from him and waved it toward Naomi. "I get another letter from *Mamm!*" she said happily.

Abe kissed the top of his daughter's head and then kissed Naomi, who'd gone to Ruthie so they could share her letter.

"I'll leave the two of you to enjoy your *mudder's* letter," Abe said to his daughters. "*Gut nacht.*"

"*Gut nacht,*" they both said at the same time.

They sat on Naomi's bed, and Ruthie started to open the letter from her mother, but her sister stopped her.

"Do you want to read the letter in private?" Naomi asked her.

Ruthie paused and looked at her quizzically. "Why would I want to read it by myself?" she asked. "You shared your letter from *Mamm* with me, and I want to share mine too. Just because our lives are changing and we are moving toward our futures does not mean we have to give up our past."

Naomi smiled at Ruthie. "You have really grown up little *schweschder;* I'm proud of you, and I'm glad we will always have *Mamm* to share between us."

"Me too," Ruthie said as she settled in close to her sister and began to read the letter aloud.

CHAPTER FIFTEEN

Ruthie shivered as she walked through the pumpkin patch selecting the pumpkins that had been protected under leaves and had not suffered from the frost last night. She was able to find seventeen so far that were unaffected; these she would take with her to town to sell to Chad for his market. The clip-clop of horse's hooves and a cold snort brought her head up toward the road. The sight of Seth made her giddy; had he come by to take her and the pumpkins into town? She giggled, and her breath puffed out in front of her like a little icy cloud against the light blue sky that wakened the morning sun that still lay on the horizon as if to say it was too early to get up yet.

Ruthie lifted an eager hand and waved to him from the middle of the pumpkin patch, and he hopped down from his closed buggy and ran toward her. She drew her mitten-clad hands to her cold cheeks and smiled as he closed the space between them and sank to one knee. He looked up at her all silly-like and smiled.

"Will you marry me?" he asked.

Ruthie giggled. "Are you going to ask me that every time you see me?"

"I might just have to until it sinks in!"

"Yes, I'll marry you!" she said with a giggle.

He jumped up and pressed his lips to hers sending a spark of warmth that made even her bones stop shivering.

"At least let me take you and your pumpkins into town," he said, still holding her close. "Were you able to spare any?"

"I don't think I'll be able to give him the full twenty-five he asked for, but I've found seventeen *gut* ones so far."

"Let's see if we can't find a few more beneath this blanket of snow!"

By the time they loaded the pumpkins in Seth's buggy, they had counted twenty-three altogether.

"We're only two pumpkins short; not bad," Seth said.

"I have two in the *haus,*" Ruthie said. "I have one on the table and one in the sitting room for decoration; we could take them to give him the full twenty-five."

Seth shrugged. "It's not that big of a deal; I doubt he'll miss two pumpkins."

"You're right," Ruthie said. "Besides, I'll need them for the seeds for next year."

"I think we could run our own farmer's market next year if you're interested," Seth offered.

Ruthie frowned. "I don't want to put Mr. Murdock out of business, and I wouldn't want to compete with him either."

"We could set it up in front of the B&B," Seth offered. "I'm sure *mei Aenti* Bess would love to have the traffic stopping in front of the B&B; it might help bring in business for her. I know her and *Onkel* Jessup had a rough year last year."

Ruthie smiled. "Sounds like a *gut* plan. You can count on me and my pumpkin patch."

Seth kissed her once more, and they were on their way to town to drop off the pumpkins. When they reached the center of downtown,

Seth asked if he could drop her and the pumpkins off and leave her and the buggy while he went across the street to the lumber yard to order a few materials to fix his barn before winter set in full swing.

Ruthie didn't mind; she took pride in knowing he would be a good provider and keep a solid roof over her head even in the winter. She watched Seth jog across the street while she went to the back and retrieved one of the pumpkins. Before she realized, Chad was on her heels grabbing the pumpkin from her.

"You're just in time!" he said. "That family waiting up there by the front is waiting for four pumpkins."

Ruthie turned to look and smiled at the kids who were eyeing the pumpkins and began to jump up and down with excitement when they saw them. "I'm afraid I only had twenty-three; the rest of them suffered last night's frost, and they have mushy spots."

He grabbed another from the back of the buggy. "I'll take what I can get."

As soon as Chad's customers left with their pumpkins, he helped her finish unloading the rest and then paid her.

Ruthie thanked him and shoved the envelope of money in her pocket, thinking that running her own farmer's market wouldn't be such a bad idea after all. Instead of getting a percentage of the take for doing all the work, they would get one hundred percent of the profits, and that sounded very good to her at the moment.

"I almost forgot," Chad said as she was getting ready to go back to the buggy to wait for Seth. "When I told my mother you'd won first prize at the bake-off, she begged me to beg you if she could have the prize-winning recipe for your whoopie pies."

Ruthie hesitated, remembering what Seth had said to her, along with their suspicions that

Robin used her bread recipe to enter the bake-off.

"I understand if you don't want to give away your recipes," Chad said sadly. "But my mother loved your bread so much; I know it would make her really happy to be able to make the whoopie pies too."

Ruthie nodded. "For your *mudder?*"

"Yes! She thinks you are the best baker in the whole county!"

Now he was buttering her up. Robin must be awfully desperate!

"Okay; do you have a piece of paper I could use to write it down on?" she asked.

Chad dashed behind the cash register and snatched up a pad of paper and a pen and handed them to her. She took them reluctantly, and she could see in his eyes he understood, but he kept quiet about it. She began to write down the recipe, wondering if Seth had been right about everything. It saddened her that someone would purposely steal from her that way, but she supposed Robin must not have a conscience—or the knowledge of God's love in her heart. Either way, she would give with a happy heart; what Chad did with it from here was between him and God. The same went for Robin.

When she finished, Ruthie bid him goodbye, but he put his hand on her arm to stop her. "Thank you," he said, moving toward her like he was going in for a hug.

She backed up and put space between them.

"I can't get a hug from my favorite partner?" he asked casually. "Without your pumpkins, I'd have lost some business today."

"I'm sorry, Chad, but I don't believe *mei* betrothed would want me to hug you—or to be partners with you, so this will be the last pumpkins from my pumpkin patch I'll bring you. You'll have to find someone else to provide pumpkins for you next year. I wish your grand *vadder* a speedy recovery; give him my best."

Chad closed his slack jaw. "You're getting married?"

"Jah," she said. "Seth asked me last night."

And again this morning!

"I wish you well also," he said quietly.

"I hope your *mudder* enjoys the whoopie pies," Ruthie said.

Chad cleared his throat as if he was distraught. "Yeah, I'm sure she will."

Ruthie waved, but Chad merely nodded, the look in his eyes making her feel even sorrier for him. She walked toward the buggy lifting a silent prayer for peace for him toward the heavens. It was a prayer that would continue for several minutes while she sat in the buggy and waited for Seth. By the time he hopped up beside her, she was deep in prayer about the recipe, regret filling her.

Seth clicked to the horse and nudged Ruthie with a kiss on her cheek, but she was still deep in thought.

"What's wrong?"

She looked at Seth, worry crowding his handsome features.

"Chad asked me—begged me—for my whoopie pie recipe."

Seth whipped his head around and looked at her. "You didn't give it to him, did you?"

She nodded. "*Jah,* I did."

"You know he's going to give it to Robin!"

"She'll have a hard time selling them without the *secret ingredient* that I left out when I wrote down the instructions!" she said with a giggle.

Seth threw his head back and laughed.

"They will be bland and tasteless," Ruthie said with a smile.

"It will serve her right if she lost customers because of it!" Seth said.

"That's not exactly what I prayed for," Ruthie admitted. "I prayed that they would have a change of heart and something *gut* would come from all of this. I forgive them both and leave it in *Gott's* hands."

Seth kissed her on the cheek. "You've got a bigger heart than I do for those *Englishers.*"

Robin came up from behind Chad and startled him. "I thought that Amish girl would never leave!" she complained. "I saw she gave you the recipe, so hand it over."

"Do you treat everyone as poorly as you treat me?" he asked. "Never mind; I already know the answer to that."

He held out the recipe but snatched it away when she grabbed for it. "I meant what I said, Robin; we're through. I don't want to see you anymore."

She laughed angrily. "You're not getting away that easily; I need more of that Amish girl's recipes."

"You'll have to find a way to get them yourself," Chad said. "She won't be bringing me anymore pumpkins or anything else ever again. She and Seth are getting married."

Robin puffed out her lower lip and mocked him. "And that makes you sad because you like her. I don't know why, but if you like her so much, break up her relationship with the Amish guy. That way, you can get me more recipes!"

Chad jutted out his chin and pursed his lips. "I will not do something so cruel, and I won't be blackmailed by you either. Please leave; I don't ever want to see you again."

"Not without that recipe!" she growled.

He let go of it when she grabbed for it and hung his head in shame.

"I'll be talking to you soon." Robin sneered at him and then walked away.

I won't be here. When I tell grandfather what I've done, he won't let me run his farmer's market anymore.

Chad spent the rest of the afternoon trying to think of what he would say to his grandfather that wouldn't make the man disappointed in him, but there was no way out of the mess he'd caused. He'd let his family down, but most of all, he'd hurt Ruthie when she'd done nothing to deserve the way he'd treated her. Not to mention the way he let

Robin hurt her. Surely, there had to be a way to fix all of this.

A text message interrupted Chad's thoughts. He lifted his phone from his back pocket and bumped off Robin's demand to come to the bakery for an emergency.

Another text followed, and another. The last one made him chuckle.

That Amish girl left out some ingredients, and the whoopie pies taste awful.

Chad chuckled harder. *Good for her!*

Another text came through. *Get over here this instant!*

Chad blew out a heavy sigh as he packed up the farmer's market and posted the *Be back after lunch* sign on the outside of the tent flap.

He walked slowly to the bakery around the corner, wondering how he was going to talk his way out of this with Robin. Lifting his head heavenward, he uttered three little words that brought him a feeling of peace he'd never felt before.

Lord, help me.

He stood outside the window of the bakery, staring at the display of Ruthie's pumpkin bread with a sign boasting it was from *an old Amish recipe.*

She's gone too far, and I need to fix this.

He entered the bakery and was surprised to see Robin's father behind the counter doing what looked like an inventory sheet. The man looked up and smiled.

"Hello, Chad," Mr. Baker greeted him. "Robin is in the kitchen."

"Mr. Baker," Chad said, with a sigh. "I have something I have to tell you."

Ruthie went to the mailbox and pulled out a large envelope addressed to her. The return address was from The Baker's Dozen Bakery. Worry filled her as she imagined a lawsuit contained in the envelope; she wouldn't put it past Robin to sue her for giving her a recipe with missing ingredients. She chuckled, trying to convince herself such a thing was preposterous.

She opened the flap and pulled out a letter, and a check addressed to her for Five Thousand Dollars.

She let out a squeal and ran up to the porch without reading the letter.

"What is it?" Seth asked.

"It's a check from Robin—*nee*—from her *dat,*" she said as she glanced at the signature on the check. She looked at the letter, which was also written by her father. "He's apologizing for Robin taking my pumpkin bread recipe and using it in the store. The check is an advance for using my recipe, and the letter is an offer for a percentage of the profits if I allow them to continue to use it."

"I wonder how he found out about it," Seth commented. "You don't suppose Chad had something to do with this, do you?"

"Judging by the look on Chad's face a couple of weeks ago when I gave him the recipe, and the prayers I've been pouring out to *Gott,* I'd be willing to bet Chad was behind this."

"If we find out he was, we'll have to thank him," Seth said.

She read more of the letter. "Mr. Baker is offering me another Five Thousand Dollars and profit sharing if I bring them the *correct* whoopie pie recipe! That Robin is one spoiled girl."

"What are you going to do?" Seth asked.

Ruthie giggled. "I'm going to give Robin the secret ingredient!"

THE END

Be sure to look for book 4 in the Amish Acres series!

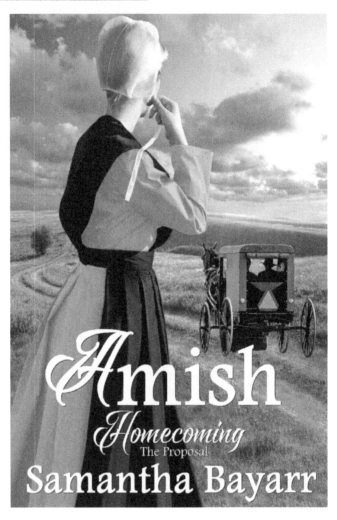

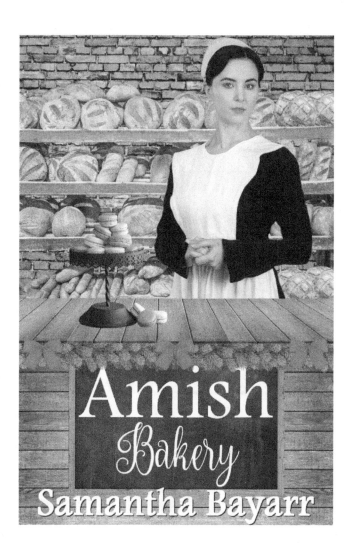

Amish
Bakery
Samantha Bayarr

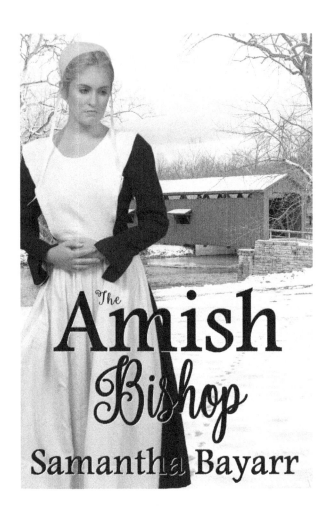

The
Amish
Bishop

Samantha Bayarr

Made in United States
North Haven, CT
11 July 2022

21187107R00136